The Pencil Bandits

Book One

To Zete

Henry Reade

By Henry Reade

With Nathaniel Reade

Published by
Henry Charles Press
London, New York, Florence

This is a work of fiction. All names, characters, places, and incidents are either products of the author's imagination or are used fictitiously, or both.

10 9 8 7 6 5 4 3 2 1

First Edition

ISBN-10: 1479393975
ISBN-13: 9781479393978

Chapter One

"I'm not eating that," said Ticonderoga. He was a skinny boy, aged eight, with neatly combed black hair. He pushed away his plate and folded his hands over his chest.

"Whath the matter?" asked his older brother, Dixon, who at age 14 had bulging muscles under his too-small Spiderman t-shirt.

"I'm not eating it."

"But it'th *fresh*!" said Dixon, who struggled to pronounce the letter 'S.' "I got it off the road mythelf!"

"Sorry, Dixon," Ticonderoga said.

"But you *like* thquirrel!" Dixon.

"How'd ya cook it, Brah?" their middle brother, Eagle, asked.

"I gently thautéed it in root beer until the tire-marks dithappeared."

"Sorry," Ticonderoga said. "I just can't any more."

"But ith your birthday!"

"I know," Ticonderoga said. "That's why you got me this."

He held up a yellowed, frayed copy of *The Wall Street Journal*.

"Do you dig it, Homey?" asked Eagle. Red-haired, aged 11, he was wearing an orange hoody sweatshirt, a straight-brimmed flat-hat, and bling.

"Oh sure," Ti said, even though he didn't. "It's just what I've always wanted."

"That's cool," Eagle said. "Cause we didn't have no greenbacks to buy you a real present. We found it in the bus shelter."

"Guys," Ti said. "I really appreciate all you've tried to do for my birthday." He pointed to the three balloons his brothers had gotten free from the East Westford Savings Bank, and a paper sign they'd found at the dump that read "Congratulations Graduates!" His father had presented him with a pillow he'd made filled with wood shavings, and a bundle of yellow Rush pencils that they'd used in the stove to heat the bus.

Ti looked at them all and sighed. "It's just that I realized something important today."

"What'th that?" Dixon asked. Ti was known for his intelligence.

"I've finally realized," Ti said, "that honesty doesn't pay."

"No, no," said their father from his bed. "It's *crime* that doesn't pay."

"Yes it does," said Eagle. "Look at Johnny Fitziguzzi."

Johnny Fitziguzzi was an old man at the nursing home who sometimes gave them money to place bets for him on the dog races. "He's rich."

"Just because he can afford an electric wheelchair doesn't mean he's rich," said their father.

"He's got more money than us," Ticonderoga said.

"That's not sayin' much, Brah."

"He's a thief!" their father said. The effort of speaking caused him to cough so much he had to lie back down in his bed.

Their father worked at the Rush Transpacific Pencil factory in downtown East Westford, Pennsylvania, but he was literally allergic to his job. He was required to load the graphite into the graphite molds, but breathing the graphite dust made him sick. He didn't get paid for sick days, and he didn't have health insurance. Their mother had died while working at the pencil factory four years ago, when a pencil flew out of a machine and into her carotid artery, killing her instantly. L. Bob Rush, the factory owner, had given the family a case of Pringles in return for their signing a legal document promising not to sue him. Then he had ordered their father back to work.

They now lived in an abandoned yellow school bus, rusty on the outside, with one remaining tire. Inside they'd made it cozy with things they had made or scrounged. The walls were beautifully decorated with pencil drawings made by their mother and Dixon, who had inherited her artistic genius.

Outside, the wheels of the bus did not go round and round. They sat on the ground of an abandoned lot on the outskirts of town. The weed trees were so high you could barely tell the bus was there, and the windows were mostly covered with cardboard. The only sign of life was the smoke that sometimes wafted out of a pipe in the roof. They heated their bus by burning reject pencils

and other wood scraps in a little stove they had made from a can. It was October, and the bus was so cold they could see their breath when they talked.

For dessert Dixon served a birthday cake made from six large pancakes stacked on top of each other and covered with maple syrup boiled down from sap he'd collected himself. They rarely had the money to buy food in a store. Sometimes they found good things to eat in dumpsters, and Dixon was an expert at hunting and foraging. These pancakes had an odd, mustardy color because he'd ground the flour himself from wild wheat berries and the yellow pollen of cat tails. In the middle of the pancake stake he'd inserted a foot-tall candle he'd found inside the nursing home.

After they'd eaten their cake, their father began coughing again, so they blew out the lamp and he went to sleep. Ticonderoga whispered to his brothers, 'See you in my office in ten minutes.' His brothers nodded in agreement.

It didn't take long to rinse off the dinner cardboard in a bucket of water they'd filled from the faucet behind the nursing home, kiss their father good night, and meet in the place Ticonderoga called his "office." It was actually a dug-out area under the bus, with walls made from scraps of wood and cardboard. To get to it they had to open the door of the bus, walk down the stairs into the cold night air, and crawl through an opening behind the right fender.

Ti was sitting at his "desk," which he'd made from a box. He was wearing his "suit," a t-shirt he pulled over his other clothes, onto which he'd drawn with a black marker a tie, jacket, and a pocket square. It was cold and dark; Dixon lit the "lamp," a piece of string in a can of fat.

Ti used the gavel he'd made from a stick and a rock to bang on his desk. "This meeting is now called to order," he said. "Are all members of the committee present?"

Eagle hated this stuff. Annoyed, he said, "Present."

Dixon, who was easily distracted, said, "What?"

Ti ignored him. "Good." He stood up and paced back and forth. He was the only one short enough to stand in the office.

"Guys," he said, "it's almost winter. And as you know, that's the hardest time for us to find food."

"Yeah," said Dixon, rubbing his head in amazement. "The animals all go somewhere."

"Florida," Eagle said. "Which is where I'd like to be chillin' right now."

"On top of that," Ti said, "It's when we need even more fuel for the stove, and Father appears to be sicker than ever, so there's going to be fewer scraps coming from the factory."

"What's left in the bank account?" Eagle said.

"Let's see." Ti pulled something from under the box that served as his desk, and held it up by the lamp. It was a clear, zip-lock bag on which someone had written in black marker, "Bank Account." He studied it for a bit, then told them, "One dollar and 17 cents."

"That won't get us through the winter," Dixon said.

"Gentlemen," Ti said, "we are in big trouble."

"Yeah. We be screwed," said Eagle.

Dixon's lip started to quiver. He was a huge boy, but he was very emotional.

Eagle gave him a pat on the back. "Don't cry, Brah."

Ti stopped pacing and looked at his older brothers. "Do either of you have any ideas?"

"How 'bout we go to the thtore!" said Dixon, cheering up.

"That's a great idea," said Ti, "except for one problem. We are completely lacking in funds."

"Fun?" Said Dixon. "We have fun!"

"*Funds,*" said Eagle. "Ya know, Brah. Like, ka-ching. Scratch. Cheese. Greenbacks. Money."

"Oh."

"Eagle," Ti asked him. "Any ideas?"

"Yeah!" Eagle said. "We make a rap video!" He jumped up, tried to do a hip-hop dance move, and bumped his head on the bus's muffler. "Ow!" He sat back down on the dirt.

"Eagle, we have discussed this before," Ti said. "It takes *money* to buy a camera, instruments, and all those dancing girls you want in the background. Our problem here isn't how to *spend* money. It's how to *get* some."

"Fine," said Eagle, rubbing his head. "If you so smart, man, let's hear your plan." He paused, then said, "Hey, that rhymes. I'm gonna use that in a tune."

"I do have a plan, as a matter of fact," Ti said. "I've been thinking about this ever since I was forced to quit my online Latin classes because we don't have an internet connection, a computer, electricity, or any other way to actually be *online*."

Ti paced back and forth, tapping into his palm one of the Faber #2s his father made by hand in his spare time for the pure love of pencils. He said, "For years now I have watched our father. He, like our mother, followed the rules. He is a rule-follower. He did the right thing. He is honest, hard-working, and decent as the day is long. His entire life he got up at dawn, went to work, did his job, 12 hours a day. And what did he get for thanks? No thanks! All he got was abuse from those hellish managers, Mr. Dietrich and Mrs. Youngs, with their insults and their time-out chairs.

"Working hard at a job, and rule-following, and doing the right thing, they tell us in school, is supposed to bring us the American Dream. But there has been no American Dream for our father. He is descended from some of the greatest pencil manufacturers in the history of the world. But look at him! He's sick, he's miserable, and he hasn't been on a vacation in 16 years."

Ti stopped pacing and pointed his finger at them. "Brothers, this has forced me to face an uncomfortable truth. Honesty is *not* the best policy. Hard work *doesn't* pay. The early bird doesn't catch the worm, and a penny saved can't be a penny earned if you haven't got a penny in the first place. As Napoleon Bonaparte once said, 'The surest way to remain poor is to be honest.'

"We all know that once I'm able to graduate from college, get my MBA, and run a hedge fund, we will be swimming in money. But until then, I don't see any alternative. It is the only way."

"What ith?" said Dixon.

"Yeah, Boo. What's the way?"

Ticonderoga got a mischievous glint in his eyes. "We have to resort to a life of crime."

Chapter Two

"Awright, Homeys, Let's go!" Eagle crawled out of the "office" and ran up into the bus. His brothers followed.

"Where are we going?" Dixon whispered, because their father was asleep now.

"You'll see," Eagle whispered back. He grabbed something off a shelf on the wall of the bus.

Dixon said, "Thath mine!"

It was his blowgun, which he'd made from a piece of plastic pipe and pencil-stub darts.

"I know," Eagle said, smiling. He headed outside, and his brothers followed him. "We gonna use it to stick up Bob's Kwikky Stop."

"No, no, no," Ti said.

"Well it'll get us chicken an' cornbread an' waffles, word."

"I don't want chicken and cornbread and waffleths, Eagle! Too many carbs."

"That's just gangsta talk, Brah," Eagle said. "I'll get you whatever you want. What do you want?"

"I don't know," said Dixon. "Filet mignon?"

"This is a terrible idea," Ticonderoga said, trying to block Eagle's path. "Don't you ever read the *East Westford Gazette?*"

Eagle said, "No."

"Well I do, and I can tell you, people who hold up convenience stores always end up in jail."

"Shut up, Shady," Eagle said, "before I cap you."

Ti pointed to the dart gun and said, "With *that*?"

Eagle's face turned red.

By the time Ticonderoga caught up with his brothers, they were already in Bob's Kwikky Stop, a little store with metal grates over the glass and gas pumps in front, across the street from the nursing home. Bob's daughter, Sheila, was behind the counter, making a green Slushy for Firechief Tony. When Tony had paid and left, Eagle walked up to her, his hood pulled down over his face. Dixon was in the corner, admiring a bag of falafel chips, a bit of drool trickling down the side of his mouth.

Sheila looked at Eagle and growled. She was nearly six feet tall, with the sleeves ripped off her pink cashier's uniform to reveal the tattoo of a skull on one large bicep and a snake on the other. She hated most things, but in particular she hated anything related to gangstas or rap music. She preferred polka. She said to Eagle, "Whataya want?"

Eagle held up the blowgun and pointed it at her. He said, "Yo, this be a robbery! Gimme all your money, honey, and five bags of them falafel chips, or I'll cap you!"

She looked at the blow gun and said, "With *that*?"

Eagle tried to look tough. "Yeah!"

Sheila bent down below the counter, and when she stood up again she was holding a sawed-off shotgun, it's barrel pointed at his head. She sneered at him. "How 'bout you cap me with that, then I cap you with this, and we see who's still alive?"

Sheila pulled the shotgun's slide back hard and cocked it.

Eagle looked nervous. Dixon tried to hide his face behind the package of pudding cups he'd been sniffing.

Time passed. Eagle stood frozen in front of the gun barrel. His legs quivered. He seemed on the verge of tears.

Then a voice behind him said, "And....Cut."

It was Ti.

Sheila looked down at him. He was that little kid who talked like a business man, tonight wearing some kind of a fake suit he'd made from a t-shirt. She said, "What did you say?"

"Cut!" Ticonderoga gave her his most adorable smile.

"Why'd you say that?"

Sheila lowered the shotgun.

Eagle, relieved, sat down on the linoleum.

"That's what directors say, my dear. When the scene is finished."

"What scene?"

"This scene. Forgive me for not introducing myself earlier. My name is Ticonderoga Faber, and these are my big brothers, Eagle and Dixon. We're filming a scene for a music video. You were excellent, by the way. You created just the sense of verisimilitude we were looking for."

"What's that?" she said.

"Reality. Realness. It was magic. You've got a certain quality the camera loves. Have you considered acting?"

"No," Sheila said, wiping her mouth with the back of her hand. "Should I?"

"I think absolutely. Let me set up an audition for you, in Hollywood."

"Hollywood, California?"

"Exactly."

"Would I get to meet Frank Sinatra?"

"Most *doubtfully*."

"Cool," she said. "I love him."

"Well," Ti said, gesturing for Dixon and Eagle to head for the door, "that's a wrap for tonight, but we'll be back to resume filming tomorrow. Will you be working, my darling?"

"I start at six," Sheila said, and winked at him.

"Excellent," Ti said. "Well, for now we'll be on our way." He pushed his brothers out the door.

He was just waving goodbye to Sheila, and breathing a quiet sigh of relief, when she raised the gun and pointed it at him. "Hold on!" she said. "You still owe me for them puddin' cups!"

Ti looked down at the floor and sighed. Dixon had abandoned two plastic cups of Yumeeze brand artificially flavored chocolate pudding, , both of them licked clean. He said, "And how much would that be?"

Sheila looked at the cash register for a very long time, squinted, pressed a button, and looked at the numbers that appeared on the top. "Dollar fifteen," she said. "Cash."

Ti handed over all the money in their plastic-bag bank account except for two pennies, tried to smile, and hurried out the door.

A few minutes later something dawned on Sheila. "Hey!" she said to Judge Lockey, a local idiot for whom she was nuking a hot dog. "That director midget didn't even have a camera!"

Chapter Three

The next afternoon after school, the Faber brothers were sitting in the room that Johnny Fitziguzzi shared at the nursing home with another old codger named Doc Roberts. It smelled like deodorant and was as messy as a tiny room could possibly be that contained nothing but two beds, two metal dressers, and a wall-mounted television. The beds were unmade, clothes lay scattered about, and on the floor was a sea of crumpled candy wrappers. When they'd gotten there Johnny, as usual, had given them a ten-dollar bill and sent them out for some Snickers bars and a bet on a dog. Today he liked Leaping Brick to win in race five.

"So you kids need advice," Johnny said, lying on his bed in a sugar coma, his face smeared with chocolate. "What is it you wanna know?"

Johnny Fitziguzzi was the closest thing the Faber brothers had to a grandfather. About 75, he had a military-style buzz-cut everywhere except the top of his head, which was bald, a white, stubbly beard, and a long white scar on the tip of his nose. He was wearing a beige jumpsuit. The big toe on his right foot emerged from a hole in his white tube-sock.

Ti had insisted that they come here. "Let's face it," he had told his brothers. "That burglary last night was a disaster. Someone could have been hurt. And now we have no money left!" He'd waved the bank-account bag at them, wit its two pennies.

"The problem," he'd told them, "is that we don't know the first thing about being criminals. And the secret to every successful career is a good teacher, to show you the ropes."

"My teacher showed me the ropes last month," Eagle said, rubbing his arm. "Then she used them to tie me to my chair."

Ti said to Johnny, "We need you to teach us how to be criminals."

"Heck, yeah," Johnny said, tearing the wrapper off another Snickers bar. "I was the greatest crook that ever lived!"

Doc snorted. A retired umbrella salesman, who was lying on his bed in a dirty yellow bathrobe, trying to watch a rerun of

Charlie's Angels on the television. He said to the brothers, "He's a complete fraud. Fitziguzzi ain't even his real name. He changed it to something he thought sounded Italian so's people would think he's a mobster."

Johnny yelled, "That's a lie! I killed Calvin Coolidge!"

"He didn't kill Calvin Coolidge. Calvin Coolidge died of a heart attack in 1933, three years before this clown was even born."

"That's not true!" Johnny yelled at Doc. They were always yelling at each other. "I killed him in a saber fight." He pointed to the scar on his nose. "That's how I got this!"

Doc rolled his eyes. "He got that from an electric can-opener, when he was drunk."

"Saber fight!"

"Drunk!"

Johnny put his fingers in his ears and yelled even louder, "Saber fight, saber fight, saber fight!"

"Go ahead," yelled Doc. "Tell these nice boys your real name. It's Coneflower!"

"Gentlemen, please," Ti said, holding up his little arms. "Let's get back to business. You *were* a criminal, right Johnny?"

"Heck yeah! You wanna see my mug shot?" Johnny pulled a wrinkled, black-and-white picture from under his pillow. It showed a man of about 30 with an army haircut, holding up a sign-board with numbers on it.

Dixon took it from him, looked at it closely, then passed it to Eagle, who said, "Das what I wanna be when I grow up."

"Good boy," Johnny said.

After they told Johnny about the previous night's stick-up attempt, Johnny waved a long, bony finger at them. "Armed robbery? That's for chumps and third-raters. They don't use real money in those stores. Didn't you know that?"

Dixon said, "What do they use?"

"Never mind that," Johnny said. "The point is, any nitwit with a pistol can walk into a store and say, 'Gimme your dough.'"

"Thath's not what Eagle said," Dixon explained. "He thaid, 'Yo, this be a robbery! Gimme all your money or I'll cap your ath!'"

Johnny pointed his Snickers at Dixon and said to Ti, "Does that big fella speak English? I mean, what the heck is a ath?"

Ti just smiled.

Johnny said, "Listen to me. Stick-ups are for amateurs."

Ti said, "So what would you suggest?"

"Oh, there's lots a nice crimes," Johnny said. "Kidnapping is good. I always liked kidnapping. You meet interesting people that way."

"But *we're* kidth," Dixon said. "Kidth can't nap kidth. Wouldn't that be bullying?"

Johnny stared at Dixon for a while. Then he said, "What planet are you from?"

Dixon said, "Earth?"

"Awright," Johnny said. "So forget the kidnapping. How 'bout hit-men? Do you like to whack people?"

"Most def'," Eagle said.

"Not really," Dixon said.

"I think we should stick to misdemeanors," Ti said. "Nowadays even children who commit felonies can get the chair."

"Good thinkin'," Johnny said. "Besides, there's a lot of upfront costs, bein' a hit man. You got your sniper rifle, your scope, your black clothes. And it can be messy. You do a lot of cleaning up. I always hated the cleaning up. I got a latex allergy. I could get a terrible rash from the rubber gloves."

"What else ya got?" Eagle asked.

"Well, when I was your age," Johnny said, unwrapping his third Snickers bar, "I had a nice little protection racket."

"Protection?" Dixon said, disgusted. "We don't wanna be protectionth! We wanna be criminalth!"

"Not like that, dummy. You don't actually protect anyone. You just make 'em *pay* protection. You say, 'Hey, gimme your lunch money and I'll make sure no bullies beat you up today.'"

"But what if they refuse to pay?"

"Then you find a bully to beat them up."

Eagle said, "Now that's a gig I'm down with, Cuz!"

"I like it," Ti said, rubbing his chin. "I like it. Dixon is strong, and Eagle is crazy. This could work perfectly. You guys?"

He looked at his big brothers, who both nodded.

Ti stood. "Well then," he said, shaking Johnny's limp old hand. "Gentlemen? Let the protection racket begin!"

Chapter Four

"I don't get it," Dixon was saying. "How come we're not going to Burr Oak?"

"Because everyone there is too tough," Ticonderoga said.

"Oh, yeah," Dixon said. "They are tough. They thteal *my* lunch money."

After a while Dixon said, "Then where *are* we going?"

"Hovering Parents," Ti explained for the third time.

"Good idea!" Dixon said. "Those hippy kids are a bunch of wimps."

Ti and Dixon were both riding inside one of those supermarket shopping carts that are made to look like a car. It belonged to Dixon. He'd gotten it for his 12th birthday from his brothers, and it was his favorite thing in the world. Dixon had somehow crammed himself into the little driver's seat, his huge head and shoulders sticking out the driver's door. Ti sat in the basket behind him. They were being pulled along by a rope that was tied to the back of Johnny Fitziguzzi's electric wheelchair, which was being slowly driven down the side of the road by Eagle.

Ti, Dixon, and Eagle all attended Burr Oak Elementary School, in East Westford. Most of the kids were so mean there that the school's mascot was the Burr Oak Bully. Ti knew they couldn't run a protection racket at Burr Oak. Hovering Parents Cooperative Community Charter School, however, was another matter. Located 12 miles up Highway 281, it attracted students whose parents could afford to own a car. They wore tie-dye and studied knitting, folk dancing, and Suzuki violin. The school allowed no screens of any kind; no phones, no televisions, no computers. The furniture was all natural, free-range, and organic. Even the toilet paper was hand-made.

After two hours of travel, Eagle pulled into the parking lot at HPCCCS. Behind a high, wooden palisade, they could hear kids singing. They found a gate, but it was locked. Finally Eagle dragged the car shopping cart over beside the fence, climbed onto its black plastic roof, and peered over the tops of the sharpened fence-posts. He said, "Yo, Boo, check this out!"

When he lifted Ti up onto his shoulders so he could see, Ti said, "This is disgusting." Instead of playing on a playground, about fifty kids in big straw hats were hoeing rows of vegetables. Under the watchful eyes of several long-haired women in loose, flowing, hempen gowns, they were all singing a horrible folk song: "Each of us is a flower, growing in life's garden. Each of us is a flower, we need the sun and rain."

"What ith going on in there?" Dixon said.

"It's ugly, Bro," Eagle said. "Those shorties be slaves."

The problem now was how to get in. All the doors and windows of the school building, which was made of mud brick and a thatched roof, were locked. They could see ponytailed security guards with radios patrolling the perimeter in tie-dyed t-shirts that said in big letters, "Well-Being Facilitator." Inside the front door, they could see a fierce-looking woman sitting at a desk. This wasn't like Burr Oak, which had no security. At Burr Oak the teachers—and probably a lot of the parents—wouldn't mind a bit if the kids were stolen.

After a few minutes of stroking his imaginary beard, Ti said, "I have an idea."

When the fierce-looking woman at the desk buzzed the three boys in the front door and looked at them, she almost called the Head Facilitator of Well-Being. They were led by a small one with neatly combed black hair, wearing a t-shirt with some sort of tie and jacket drawn onto it. He was followed by a taller one in sagging jeans, orange, hooded sweatshirt, and one of those flat hats the hip-hop hoodlums liked to wear. Behind them, lumbering like a football player, was a huge boy wearing raggedy jeans and a Spiderman t-shirt that was much too small for him. They looked to her like a gang of child hobos.

"Can I help you gentlemen?" she snarled at them, her finger on the buzzer that would instantly and silently alert the Well-Being Facilitators.

"Yes!" said the little one. He smiled at her so charmingly that she almost smiled back. He was adorable. "We have an appointment to perform today."

"And who might you be?"

"You don't recognize us?" Ti said and smiled again, revealing the dimples in his cheeks. "We're the Tonsils. We're one of the most famous theater groups in the country."

Eagle, who hadn't been listening, said, "Actually we a most def, supa bad rap group. We called Fo Shizzle!" He busted a few made-up gang signs.

"Which is it?" the woman said.

"Well," said Ti, shooting Eagle a dirty look, "my brother's right. We're all of those things. We're a theatrical group, and a musical group. Musical theater! Our goal is to interpret the urban experience for over-protected youth."

"How fascinating," the woman said as if she almost meant it. She had opened an appointment book and was pointing to a page. "But I don't see you in the book."

"How could that be?" Ti said, sounding outraged. He turned to his brothers. "Can you believe this, boys? After travelling all this way?"

"We come from New York City, Sista," Eagle said. "That's a long drive."

"But you're not in the book!"

"This's typical," Eagle said, "of how we exploited by The Man."

"Yeah," said Dixon.

"There must be some mistake," Ti said. "I arranged this appointment personally, with Headmaster Gary." Before they'd come here, Ti had spent some time on the computer in the library, collecting names of important people at HPCCCS.

"But Headmaster Gary is in Botswana, teaching the children to fish."

Ti knew that, too. "I see," he said. "So Headmaster Gary failed us. This is a grave insult to my people."

"I'm gon tell the President!"

"Hold on now, hold on," said the woman. "There's no need for that. The performance space is in the Eatery, and the children are there now, sharing lunch. It's right through those wooden doors. I'll buzz you through."

The Eatery smelled skunky, like steamed cabbage. Under the watchful eye of adult monitors strumming harps, the kids sat on woven mats on the dirt floor, eating green sludge from wooden bowls.

"All right," Ti said. "Here they are. Our first victims. Let's work it!"

The three of them sat down next to a circle of kindergarteners.

Dixon sniffed at the sludge in a black-haired boy's bowl. "What ith that crap?"

"What's cwap?" said the boy.

"Thith!" said Dixon, licking a finger he'd poked into the bowl.

"No it's not," said a smarty-pants girl with blonde dreadlocks. "We grew it ourselves. It's ground kale."

"Dithguthting," Dixon said. "I'd rather eat the ground. Why didn't you thauté it in garlic and butter, and maybe some nice Thpanish sausage? Then it'd be edible."

"Because we're *vegans*," the smarty-pants said. "We know butter is poisonous. It causes mucous. *Raw* kale is very high in minerals."

"So ith the ground."

"Now listen up, Vanilla. Here's how this deal is gonna go down." Eagle glared at the kids. "We be gangstas, you dig? An' we here to protect you. Every week, every one a you little whitey punks gonna pay us protection money. Got it?"

"To protect us from what?" said a boy with hair down to his shoulders. "Aren't the Well-being Facilitators here to protect us?"

"Na, they here to oppress you. We gonna protect you from bullies."

"Bully is *bad*," said the smarty-pants girl.

"Fo' shizzle it is, and that's why you gonna *pay*. Now every one a you little punks gonna pay us twenny-five cents every week, otherwise some bully gonna shank you."

A long-haired boy asked, "Will you protect us from the Castelli?"

"What the hell is a Castelli?" Eagle demanded.

"Monsters."

"Mean to us."

"Yeah, sure," Eagle said. "We'll protect you from the Castellis, and any other gang. But first you gotta pay."

"Okay!" The boy pulled a hand-knitted pouch hanging on a string around his neck from under his shirt and removed a quarter.

Eagle smiled at him. He'd covered two teeth with tinfoil, hoping they looked like grillz. The sight of them made two of the girls start to cry. "All right now, the rest a you shorties, pay up!"

As they were leaving the Eatery, their pockets jingling with quarters, the brothers heard the black-haired boy talking to one of the adult monitors while he scraped the remains of his green sludge into a compost bin full of worms.

"I know what this is called!" the boy said to the grown-up.

"What's that, Precious?" the woman asked.

"It's called *cwap!*"

Chapter Five

Eagle was parking Johnny Fitziguzzi's electric scooter in front of the nursing home when they saw him through the glass doors inside the foyer. The door of one of the metal mailboxes that lined a wall of the foyer was hanging open, the lock slightly bent, envelopes and junk mail on the floor. The brothers could see a big screwdriver sticking out of Johnny's back pocket. He didn't notice them at first, outside the glass, because he was busily tearing open envelopes and muttering to himself, "Where the hell's the cash? Old Lady Rogers always gets cash on her birthday."

"Hey Brah!" Eagle rapped on the glass and yelled to him.

"What?" Johnny Fitziguzzi jumped, and tried to hide the envelopes behind his back. When he saw it was them he relaxed. He opened a fire-exit door and let them in. "Hello there. I was just tidying up." He dropped the envelopes on the floor.

Eagle flashed some made-up gang signs and said joyously, "We dids the gig!"

"What's a gig?"

"Y'know," Eagle said. "We busted on them shorties over to the Charter School, jus' like you said. We bees in the rackets now. We made thirteen hundred dollah!"

Johnny Fitziguzzi looked at Eagle for a bit, mystified, then turned to Ti. "Translate for the kid, will ya?"

"We've begun a protection service, over at Hovering Parents Cooperative Community Charter School," Ti explained, "just as you suggested." He held up a plastic bread bag, containing about a pound of nickels, dimes, and quarters. "And we actually made $12.75. Plus the lollipop that kid with the runny nose gave us."

"Turned out it was already half eaten," Dixon said. "That wath dithguthtin. Next time I see that kid I'm gonna pinch him."

"Twelve-seventy-five?" Johnny said. "Not bad, kid, not bad. I remember my first protection racket. The nuns didn't wanna pay, but they changed their tune once the rocks started comin' in the windows and the broken glass started hittin' the orphans."

"Kareemy!" Eagle said.

Johnny eyed the bag of change, licked his lips, and smiled at them. "'Course, I get half."

"Half?" Eagle said. "*Half? That's like, twelve bucks!*"

"It's six dollars and 37 cents," Ti said.

"Six dollars, thirty-seven and a *half* cents," Johnny corrected him.

"We can give you five percent, Mister Fitziguzzi," Ti said. "For use of the wheelchair."

"Five?"

"Plus we'll throw in worldwide film rights and a Oh Henry bar."

"Two Oh Henrys and you got a deal."

After they'd bought the candy bars and given Johnny his take they had just over ten dollars left.

"We've got just over ten dollars left," Ti said.

"Let's get us some 45s," Eagle said.

"Guns?" Ti said. "You can't buy guns for ten bucks."

"I'm not talkin' about *burners*, Homey," Eagle said. "I'm talkin' about some Colt 45s. Some malt liquor. Some beverage."

He grabbed the bag of change away from Ti and started walking towards Bulletproof Liquors and Check Cashing, on the corner of Ivy and Vine. It looked like a fortress, with its metal gates over the windows and doors.

"No!" Ti called after him. "We need to *invest* it! My accounting teacher at the church was telling me about a new tech stock called Sefinex that's only two dollars a share, but when their laser oven gets approved it's definitely going to five hundred!"

"No way," Dixon said. He was so big that it took him about five strides to catch up with Eagle, twist his arm, and remove the bag of money from his fist. "We need to get Daddy allergy medicine. And altho a filet mignon."

"Fish Filet?" Eagle said, excited. "Like they got at Chubby Dave's? Them's good!"

"No, thilly," Dixon said. "That'th full of partially hydrogenated cotton-theed oil and corn bloatner. I could thauté us up a nice monkfish, but I wanna get our Daddy filet *mignon*. He needs B-12 and iron."

Forty minutes later they emerged from Wally World Discount Warehouse, fighting over one plastic shopping bag.

"Gimme the chips," Eagle was saying. "An' I want my Red Bull."

"No," Dixon was saying, trying to keep the bag away from him. "The Doritos are for dethert, and we agreed to *share* the Red Bull."

"Fine," Ticonderoga said, annoyed, and crossed his arms over his little chest. "We'll just have to buy stock with next week's take."

The following Wednesday, a cloudy, warm day, the three brothers returned to Hovering Parents Cooperative Community Charter School. This time, however, they'd brought a ladder, woven from sticks and plastic they'd found in the dumpster behind the nursing home. Dixon tossed one end of the ladder up over the palisade walls that surrounded the school's gardens until a section of it caught on the spiked tops. Ti went first, because he was the lightest, but Dixon had woven the bags so well that they supported even his bulk.

When the three brothers dropped down into the bushes on the other side of the fence they saw about 40 third-graders weeding plants with hoes. The adults in their flowing dresses were banging drums and leading the song. "Each of us is a flower," the kids mumbled like robots, "growing in life's garden. Each of us a flower, beneath the sun and rain."

"When I hear your sniffling," the adult holding the guitar said to one child when they were done singing, "it sounds to me like you need more practice. Let's try it again, but louder this time, shall we? And remember to kill the weeds on the downbeat."

"Madam Starflower?" said a little boy with braids down to his waist. "Isn't killing bad?"

"Not if they're weeds, Arabel," the woman with the guitar said. "Now sing!"

"Jeeze," Eagle said to Dixon from their hiding place behind the tool shed. "I'd rather be in the slamma."

When the kids finished with "Farm Hour," as it was called, they were required to bring their hoes and rakes back to the tool shed. As they did Dixon leapt out and grabbed the first one, a chubby fellow in a purple dress and beads. He pulled him behind the shed, where Eagle threatened him with a sharpened pencil.

"Your weekly payment is due," Ti said to him, smiling.

"What'd you have for lunch today?" Dixon demanded.

"Tempeh!" the boy said. "With yeast!"

"Pay up, Shorty," Eagle said, waving the pencil under his chin, "or I cut ya with my shiv."

"Wait a second," Ti said. "What happened to your face?"

Dixon's mouth hung open. "It'th *beautiful.*"

The side of the boy's face and neck was covered with the kind of tattoos you'd see on a Polynesian tribesman: geometric patterns of yellow, red, and orange, with the head of a realistic green snake emerging from under his shirt and wrapping around his neck.

The boy started to sniffle. "You promised us!" he said. "You said you were gonna protect us from the Castelli! But look what happened!" He pulled down the back of his tunic to reveal a beautiful image of the snake's coils strangling a teacher. "It didn't work! And I'm gonna tell!"

They looked out from behind the shed and noticed that many of the other kids also had drawings on their faces, arms, and legs.

Eagle looked fierce. "Don't you worry, Shorty. This be *my* hood now, an' me an' my Bloods, we gonna take *down* these Castellis."

"Where would we find the Castellis?" Ti said sweetly. "I'm sure we can make them see reason."

"After school," the boy said. "In the drumming amphitheater. Before the Parental Responsibility Transfer. That's when the Castelli gets us." He hid his face with hands. His hands, the brothers noticed, were covered with artfully drawn images of the Hovering Parents Cooperative Community Charter School, in flames.

Chapter Six

Ti called a meeting inside the garden shed to prepare them for battle. Along the shed's walls hung hoes, shovels, and rakes in neat, carefully labeled racks. Chickens clucked and cooed in the back corner. If anyone had tried to keep chickens at Burr Oak, Ti thought, they'd have long since become somebody's supper.

Dixon was inspecting the bunches of dried herbs that hung from the rafters.

"Thavory?" he said, sniffing at a bundle of dried savory. "Thweet! And ith that lemon grass? I am so doing a Thai Curry once I get a can of cocoanut milk."

"Dixon!" Ti called to him. "This meeting is now called to order."

"Okay," Dixon said. He shoved bundles of herbs into his jeans pockets and sat down on a wooden wheelbarrow.

"Gentlemen," Ti said. "And you too, Eagle."

Eagle didn't smile.

"That was a joke."

"Yeah, yeah."

Ti continued. "This is the first time we will go into battle as a family, and it sounds as if we are facing a fearsome gang of toughs. So we need to work together, for the first time in our lives. No more everybody going off in his own direction, like that time you saw a puppy and left all those groceries on the sidewalk and they got stolen."

"Hey!" Eagle said. "That puppy was *cute*."

"We've got great potential here, guys," Ti continued. "My brain, of course. Dixon's strength. And Eagle?"

"I got my sharpened-pencil shivs!"

"Tremendous. But we have to work together, as a team."

"Yeah, yeah," Eagle said. "Cut to the chase, will ya Brah?"

Ti gave Eagle a look. "So I have worked out a plan." He unrolled a map which he'd drawn on a bag that had formerly contained organic fertilizer. The map showed the layout of the school grounds. "Because we'll probably be outnumbered, I have employed an attack plan that was once used to excellent effect by Subutai, the greatest Mongol general who ever lived. The Mongols always faced larger armies, and they always won, thanks in large part to their superior tactics. Of course, it didn't hurt that they were often drunk on fermented horse milk."

"Yeah," Eagle said. "Gimme some!"

"In one of Subutai's greatest battles, against the Kipchaks, he enticed the opposing army to pursue him, thinking they had him defeated. They followed him into a deep cavern, where his siege engines rained down rocks from above. Then his light cavalry rode in and sliced them to pieces."

"What's a thiege engine?" Dixon asked.

"A catapult? A trebuchet? Later they even used primitive cannon."

"Yo, Brah," Eagle said. "Tha's kareemy."

"So this is what we will do," Ti said. "I'll act as the decoy. I will go out to face the Castellis, and taunt them with insulting language. I will call them horrible, vile names, such as scalawags, cuss-buckets, and procrastinators. They will see my small size, but not my superior intelligence. They will follow me to here."

He pointed to a spot on the map behind the Weaving Hall. "Eagle!"

"Yes sir!" Eagle gave him an enthusiastic salute.

"You will be waiting for them on the roof of the Hall. You will drop down on them like the bird of prey you're named for."

"I thought he wath named for a pencil."

"You will use your pencil swords to quickly stab the enemy in the ankles and shoulders, thus causing the utter destruction of their morale."

"Fo' sure, Boo! I'm gonna mess them up."

"And what do I do?" Dixon asked.

"You, my gentle behemoth, will charge in from behind like Hannibal's elephants, cutting off all their hope of escape. Then you will pummel them about the face and stomach. I, meanwhile, will be like Subutai's siege engines. I will pelt them with rocks and garbage and anything else I can find. Finally, the three of us will converge on the center, laying waste to the Castellis until they beg for our forgiveness. Agreed?"

"Agreed," Dixon said.

"Fo' shizzle!" Eagle said.

"Eagle," Ti said as they left the shed, "you do realize that you're not African-American?"

"Hey, Brah," Eagle said. "You cain't tell a comic book by its cover."

At 5:15 by the sun dial in the courtyard, the enrichment programs finally ended and someone banged the Tibetan prayer gong four times. The brothers could see Volvos, Priuses, and Lexus station-wagons lining up in the Parental Responsibility Exchange Circle.

Over by the Drumming Amphitheater, Ti saw children shrieking, then running away from something. He grabbed one of them as she passed and asked what was the problem. She said, "It's the Castelli!"

Ti waved his red handkerchief at his brothers, who were both in position, the pre-arranged signal that let them know he was going in. He walked slowly towards the center of the commotion. He was smiling.

When he got closer to the front doors, Ti didn't see the gang. He kneeled down by a boy who was hiding behind a bush and said, "Excuse me. Can you tell me where I might find the Castellis?"

"Right there," the boy said. He sounded like he might cry. "Right there!"

He pointed to an area by the Stonehenge sculpture.

Ti said, "All I see is a girl."

"Yeah!"

"Where are the rest of them?"

"Whataya mean?" the boy said. "That's *it*. That's the menace right there!"

The girl started walking towards them.

"Run!" the boy said. "Run for your life!" He scurried away.

'This is gonna be easy,' Ti thought to himself. She looked like she was about 14, with black hair she'd gelled into spikes. She was wearing red, high-top sneakers, a black leather jacket, and jeans spattered with paint and oil. 'There's just one of them,' he thought, 'and she's a girl.'

When the girl was about ten feet away, Ti yelled, "You're apathetic!"

"What?" She kept getting closer. Ti began to back up.

"And you're indifferent!"

"Huh?" She came closer.

He backed up faster, and let her really have it. *"And,* you're also a *stinky pants!"*

"You take that back."

"You wanna try and make me?"

"Yeah," she said. When he started to run, she followed. The plan was working.

Ti lured her into the courtyard by the Weaving Hall, then hid behind its far wall. While the girl looked around, Eagle dropped off the low roof and pulled two pencils from the pockets of his hoody, which he'd sharpened to pinpoints.

He yelled, "Hit the wall and spread, pretzel-head! See, I'm a poet, and don't you know it."

The girl looked at him for a while, with his orange hoody, flat hat, and the waistband of his baggy jeans hanging down below his butt. She noticed that the so-called bling around his neck was made of gold plastic. The side of her lip began to curl into a smirk.

Eagle looked mystified. He said, "Yo, you heard what I said, girl! Hit the dirt! Or I make the blood squirt!"

"With what?" She was staring at him, the smirk getting bigger.

"With my shivs, Fool!"

"Oh yeah?" The girl reached behind her back and pulled something from inside her jacket. "Well I'd like your shivs to meet my friends here, Maim and Kill."

She unfolded a pair of black nunchuks and began spinning one of the wooden sticks over her head like the blade of a helicopter.

Eagle figured he had to do something—he was, after all, a gangsta—so he lunged at her with the pencils. The girl stepped forward, the nunchuks whirred around his ears and arms, and something went crack crack.

When she'd stepped back Eagle was holding a broken stub in each hand.

"Oh yeah, yo?" Now Eagle was mad. He reached behind *his* back, and pulled something from *his* waistband. He waved them at her.

Two more super-sharp pencils.

"I don't wanna have to do it to a cutie like you with the smokin' hot booty ooo ooo," he said, "But if I have to I will carve you. More poetry."

Again the nunchuks whirred, air swarmed around his body, and he heard two cracks. When he looked down he saw two more broken stubs in his hands.

Eagle pulled out another pair, this time from his left sock.

Again she spun the nunchuks and snapped them both in two.

Eagle patted his chest. He felt something in his shirt pocket. He reached in and pulled out two more pencils, which he pointed at her.

Whir, swoosh, snap, snap.

"Hey!" he said in a normal, non-gangsta voice. "Those were bonded-graphite Tri-Writes! These things are expensive! Now surrender!"

"Why?" She smiled at him.

"'Cause I'm all out of pencils?"

"Then it's time for you to hit the dirt, squirt, before I make your body really hurt."

"Wow," Eagle said. "Nice rhymes." He lay down, put his hands behind his head, and wove them together.

Ti had been watching this from the roof of the Weaving Hall. Things hadn't gone quite as planned. He didn't see any reason to shell her with the few pebbles and acorns he'd found. What was the point? He did, however, still have a secret weapon, which was half a foot taller than her, and a good 50 pounds heavier.

"Dixon!" he yelled. "Attack!"

The girl noticed Ti on the roof, then looked behind her to where Dixon stood.

She spun the nunchuks over her head and said to him, "You want a taste, Incredible Hulk?"

"No!" Dixon yelled.

He was just standing there, gazing at her like she was an angel. He was in love.

But it wasn't mutual.

The girl spun the nunchucks over her head and lunged. The stick tore a hole out of the corner of his t-shirt.

Dixon looked like he might cry. "You hurt my betht Thpidey shirt!"

"She hurt your only Spidey shirt," Eagle said.

Dixon took the next whack to the side of his large head. He collapsed onto Eagle, who grunted. The girl jumped on top of him and stuck her knee into the back of Dixon's neck. She had both brothers pinned.

By now the Charter School students had formed a ring around them, and most of them were chanting, "Kill them! Kill them! Kill them!"

Some were more specific. A boy who wore a hand-carved wooden cross on leather thong around his neck screamed, "Pull out their eyeballs! Pull out their eyeballs and light them on fire! Pull out their eyeballs, light them on fire, and make them eat the ashes!"

The girl with blonde dreadlocks yelled, "Somebody call the dopes!"

Another kid picked up a phone mounted to the outside of the palisade and yelled, "Help! Help! Conflict in the Enrichment Area!"

Ti, meanwhile, had jumped down from the low roof of the Weaving Hall and come to stand by the girl. He smiled at her, as if he was the sweetest person on the planet.

She said, "Who are you?"

"My name's Ticonderoga," he said. "Did you do that beautiful artwork on those kids?"

"Yeah," she said. "It's a hobby of mine."

"You're extremely gifted," he said. "Some of the images reminded me of Paul Gauguin, during his Tahitian phase."

"Really?" she said. "I like him. I was going more for late Picasso, but I can see the Gauguin influence for sure."

"And your name is Castelli?" He noticed a gold crown tattooed on her forearm.

"Yeah."

Ti pointed to the squirming bodies below her knee. "Those are my brothers."

"Oh." She stood up. Dixon rolled off of Eagle, but they both just lay there.

She looked down at Ti. "So you must be the midget who told these kids you could protect them from *me.*"

"Uh, yeah."

"Well forget it, kid. I handle the crime around here. If anyone's gonna run a protection racket, it's gonna be *me.*"

"Kill them!" the students around them were yelling. "Why don't you kill them?"

"Reach down their throat and stick a grenade where their kidney should be!" yelled the boy with the wooden cross.

"I could kill you," Castelli said to Ti, "but for some reason I like you. So I'm gonna let you off easy. I expect you to come back here one week from today, pay me every single quarter you collected from these sniveling little worms, plus another fifty bucks aggravation fee. And for every week you're late, it doubles. I know exactly how much you took from my customers, so I'm expecting $62.75. If you don't pay up, I will hunt you down and let my friends here, Maim and Kill, break every bone in your butt. You got that?"

Ti reached out his hand. "You've got a deal, Ms. Castelli."

"It's just Castelli."

They heard sirens. Three bearded men in tweed jackets and corduroy pants rounded the corner on big-wheeled tricycles. On the fronts of their helmets it said "D O P E," for "Department of Psychological Education."

The first man switched off the siren, got down from his trike and said, smiling, "What's the nature of the conflict?"

Castelli said to him, "Shut up."

"Have you forgotten the five rules of success?" the second man asked her, also smiling.

"Honesty, loving, caring, sharing, and respect!" said the third.

Dixon said, "What?"

"Nobody ever succeeded with that crunk," Eagle said.

"We better get out of here," Ti said to his brothers. "Before they make us hug."

The Charter School kids, however, were still yelling, "Kill them! Kill the thieves! Bash in their brains with the sticks!"

"No no, Wintergreen," one of the bearded men said to the boy with the cross around his neck. "You know better than that. What have we taught you?"

"I know," Wintergreen said.

"What?!"

"Killing is bad because it hurts feelings."

"Very good."

As the Dopes escorted the four of them to the exit, Ti spoke quietly to Castelli. "Can I ask you a question?"

"Yup."

"What the hell are *you* doing here?*"

"That, little man," Castelli said, putting her leather-gloved hand on his shoulder, "is a question I ask myself every day."

Chapter Seven

Johnny Fitziguzzi was on his bed, playing with a pair of dentures. "Them are nice," he was shouting at Ticonderoga. Johnny's roommate, Doc, was lying on his bed watching the Home Shopping Channel on the little TV mounted on the wall. The room wasn't much bigger than a closet, and the TV was so loud Johnny had to shout. "See these teeth?" he said, tapping one with his yellowy fingernail. "That's the good stuff. That's Swiss."

"Are those yourth, Mister Fitziguzzi?" Dixon asked.

"Heck no," Johnny said, grinning to reveal a mouth full of what looked like yellow corn kernels. "These are my own original choppers. Ya wanna know why they look so good? 'Cause every day, first thing in the morning, I gargle with vodka. The real stuff, not that crap from Connecticut."

"So then," Ti asked, pointing to the dentures, "what are you doing with those?"

"These? I boosted 'em from old lady Saffoon while she was snoozing in the day room. Slipped 'em right out of her mouth!"

"What for?" Ti asked.

"What for?" Johnny Fitziguzzi said, as if Ti was an idiot. "A guy's gotta make a living, don't he? I'm gonna wait 'til she offers a reward, then I'm gonna just happen to *find* 'em in the cafeteria and collect. Last week I did a hundred bucks on hearing aids."

"Yo Johnny," Eagle said.

"Mista Fitziguzzi to you, punk," Johnny said, and pointed a bony finger at him. "Only the midget gets ta call me Johnny."

"Okay, *Mister* Fitziguzzi. Yo, we gots a problem. We needs a serious stack of greens."

"What, spinach?"

"Greenbacks, Mister Fitziguzzi. You know, money."

"What's with this kid? How come he don't speak English?"

"The protection racket didn't go so well, Mister Fitziguzzi," Ti said.

"Please. Call me Johnny."

"We ran into a roadblock."

"And she was thuper cute," Dixon said.

"And in order to satisfy this road block we need to come up with another 62 dollars and 75 cents."

"Oh, I get it," Johnny said. "You got yourself a little girlfriend, you wanna take her out, treat her nice, maybe place a couple of bets for her at a cock fight."

"Sure," Ti said. It would have been too embarrassing to explain that the three of them had been beaten by one girl.

"We gotta come up with a whole lot of dollars," Dixon said. "And quick."

"Why don't you get a job?" yelled Doc, the roommate, from the other bed. He was staring at a bracelet made of fake diamonds on the TV.

Johnny waved him off. "Jobs are for sheep," he yelled. "JFK had a job, look how he ended up. Ted Williams had a job, and you don't see him around anymore, do ya?"

"You had a job," Doc said.

"Did not."

"Did too."

"Did not."

Did too."

"Did not! Did not! Did not!"

"Yeah you did," Doc said. "You were the assistant manager of a KFC for 26 years."

"That's a damned lie!"

"I seen the pension checks."

"A lousy 39 bucks a month. That money-grubbin' Scrooge of a colonel played me for a fool."

"Please, Johnny," Ti said, giving Johnny his most wide-eyed, adorable smile. "We need to find a way to make 62 dollars and 75 cents. And we need to do it soon!"

"Awright, fine," Johnny said. "But finding the criminal enterprise that's right for you ain't easy, ya know. It's not like buyin' a pair of bowling shoes. It takes time." He cocked his head to the side and thought for a minute. "I know, I know. Here's what you wanna do."

"What's that?"

"This is good. You're gonna like this."

"Yo, what is it, Brah?"

"I ain't no bra. I'm a man."

"What's your idea, Johnny?"

"This I gotta hear," said Doc.

Johnny ignored him. "You got a crew. There's three of ya. So here's what you wanna do. You wanna boost yourself a tractor trailer."

"To live in?" Dixon said. "But what about our buth?"

"No, no, you don't live in it, dummy. You liberate it. You hijack it, you take it somewhere, you pull out the stuff, you fence it, you pocket the cash. Badabing, you got your 63 clams."

"What do you mean, 'fence it,'" Ti asked.

"Unload it. Sell it. You know. Through your fence."

"We don't got no fence," Eagle said. "We got a bus."

"You guys are the dumbest criminals I ever met. Not that kinda fence, dimwit. A fence like Trenchcoat Jimmy, the guy who used to sell fake Rolexes down by the pool hall. A guy who takes the stuff that you liberated and sells it for you."

"He helps you stick it to The Man!" Eagle said. "And fight the power!"

"Yea, whatever." Johnny took a swig from a pint bottle of apricot brandy he kept hidden in his sock, and noticed that the kids still looked confused. "Take for instance this wise guy I knew back in Newark, name of Louie. He boosted a truck, he opens up the back, it's filled top to bottom with them 'I Love New York' t-shirts. Musta been six hundred in there. He takes 'em to Trenchcoat Jimmy, and Jimmy gives him two bucks each. So how's he doin'? He's doin' pretty good, cause now he's got twelve hundred bucks. He buys himself a 80-foot yacht, now he's livin' on the beach in Boca Raton!"

"In your dreams," Doc muttered.

"Keep it up, smart guy," Johnny said to Doc, "and you just might find your adult diapers full of holes again."

Doc shrunk back into his pillows.

Eagle was hopping around, excited. "Fo' shizzle, yo! This plan be da bomb."

"Heh?" Johnny said to Ti, hooking his thumb towards Eagle.

"He likes it," Ti said.

"Oh good," Johnny said sarcastically. "That puts my mind at ease."

"But yo yo yo," Eagle said, busting a few hip-hop moves. "Check it out. What if we goes and boosts somepin even better than t-shirts."

"Like what?"

Eagle was smiling, his eyes huge. "Like . . . puppies!" He had a thing for puppies.

"Eagle, we've been through this so many times before. We can't afford a puppy. We can't even afford to feed ourselves."

"But yo, Brah, check this out. Do you know how much you can get for just one thoroughbred Teacup Maui Sheepdog?"

"How much?"

"Like, eleven hundred large!"

Even Johnny Fitziguzzi was impressed with that number. "That's a lotta scratch."

"Fo' shizzle it is, Brah!" Eagle rubbed his hands together. "Okay, let's get started. Ti, you go find the truck. And make sure it's got Teacup Maui Sheepdogs, right Brah? I don't want no yuppie Labradoodles."

He turned to Dixon. "You, Brah. You gotta get to work practicing your stick-up voice."

Dixon looked confused. "What do I thay?"

"Whataya think, Stupid? You say, 'Yo, homey, this a stick-up, yo. Gimme the puppies or I bust a cap in you.' Now let's go!"

Eagle pulled Dixon onto his feet and started him towards the door. Then he noticed that Ti was still sitting on the edge of the bed, his little arms folded over his chest.

"What?" Eagle said. "What's wrong?"

"Where should I start?" Ti said. "First of all, how are we going to find a truck filled with thoroughbred Teacup Maui Sheepdogs? Do you honestly think that miniature thoroughbred dogs are shipped around the country in tractor-trailer trucks?"

"I don't know." Eagle thought for a second. "Yes!"

"And even if we did find such a truck," Ti continued, "How do we steal it?"

"I already explained that," Eagle said. "Dixon goes up to the guy who's driving it and says, 'Yo, homey, this a stick-up! Gimme the puppies or I bust a cap in you.'"

"But we don't have a gun," Ti said. "We can't bust a cap in him."

"You don't want no stinkin' gun on a armed robbery," Johnny said. "A gun can get you twenty-five in the Big House."

"Well then why would he give us the truck? Because we look scary?"

Eagle was pouting. "Maybe."

"And three," Ti said, "even if he did give us the truck, none of us can drive."

"Yo Ti," Eagle said, "you are always thinking negative. You're always crushing my dreams." He pointed his finger at Ti. "Puppies are da *bomb*, yo. Puppies are better than *kids*."

"I'm a kid," Dixon said. "How ith a puppy better than me?"

"Puppies are better because they don't crush your dreams, yo," Eagle said. "Puppies aren't negative. Puppies are better because no matter how stupid or ugly or poor or mean you are, puppies will still *love* you."

"And a puppy will never try to steal your truck," Ti said.

"Yeah, Brah," Eagle said. "Now you got it."

"Aw right, aw right," Johnny Fitziguzzi said. He wiped apricot brandy from his lip. "Here's what ya wanna do. Maybe the kid's right. You couldn't even run a decent protection racket, boostin' a truck is way over your heads. You gotta boost somethin' small. *Ease* into it. That way you can try it out, see if boostin' is for you. See if it's a good fit. That's what life is all about, really. Findin' the illegal activity that's right for you."

"Like what?" Ti asked.

"Like, you go down to Wally World, you boost me a couple a them jumbo Sugar Boom bars I like. You bring 'em back here, I give you a buck. See if you like it."

"Yeah!" Eagle said. "Then we only have to do it 62 more times and we'll have the money for Castelli!"

At the sound of her name, Dixon got a dreamy look. "I like her hair."

"Okay," Ti said to Johnny. "That'll work. We can do that."

"Let's go!"

"Hold on, Eagle," Ti said. "First we need to come up with a plan."

"Not another plan. They take tho long." Dixon rubbed his round belly. "I'm hungry. Mister Fitziguzzi?" he said, "Can you thmuggle us into the dining room?"

"You gonna steal me them Sugar Boom bars, like a good boy?"

"Sure we are, Mister Fitziguzzi," Ti said.

"Okay kid," Johnny said. "Okay."

Chapter Eight

"This be *dope*, yo!" Eagle whispered to his brothers. He was talking about a bowl of applesauce he held in his hands.

"I like it better with a dash of thinnamon," Dixon said.

Johnny Fitziguzzi's face appeared under the tablecloth. "Keep it down under there," he hissed. "You want I should get busted?"

As he did on special occasions, Johnny had smuggled them into the small, dark cafeteria where he took his meals. He did this by putting all three boys onto Doc's wheelchair and covering them with a blanket so that only Dixon's face showed at the top, and Eagle's huge gold basketball sneakers showed at the bottom. Once he'd wheeled them to his usual table, they would slide under the red vinyl cloth that covered it and wait there in the dark. When he could, Johnny would hand them plates and bowls of soft, gray food he managed to swipe from the other residents' trays.

"Check her out, Billy!" they heard Johnny say to one of his table-mates. "It's that chicky you like."

"Where?" Billy asked in a tired voice.

"Up on the TV! CSI Des Moines! The red-head!"

"Where?" Billy said again. While he was looking at the screen mounted to the far wall of cinderblock Johnny nabbed his creamed corn, lifted the tablecloth, and shoved it at them. Ti grabbed the bowl and slurped it down.

Three hours later, their stomachs delightfully full, the Faber brothers stood outside the biggest Wally World in East Westford. Before they were born, their father told them, their town didn't have any Wally Worlds. It had small stores on Main Street with names like "bakery" and "butcher shop," where people went in and bought what they wanted directly from a person—sometimes the actual owner. Then the Wally World had come, promising discount prices, and grown bigger and bigger, until gradually all the little shops had closed and their owners had gone broke and moved away. Those shops had paid taxes, but for some reason the Wally World didn't have to, making the town even more poor. The streets were now full of potholes so big in some places that entire cars had fallen into them. Main Street was just two rows of grafittied plywood where the windows had been. And the Wally World, in the far corner of town, was about the only place where you could buy anything, from baby formula to coffins.

As usual, Ti had concocted a complex plan. "This one," he had said while drawing it out for them on a scrap of paper, "is based on the Normandy Invasion. As you know," he explained while Dixon and Eagle grew progressively more sleepy, "Eisenhower had General Patton create an enormous diversionary force in Britain, to the north of Normandy. This fooled the Germans into thinking that the invasion would be in northern France. Instead the Allies invaded to the south. The Germans kept their best armies in the north for three days, thinking the main assault was still coming, thus giving the allies time to establish the beachhead that eventually won the war."

Eagle's eyes were now closed, his chin slumped on his chest.

Ti yelled in his ear. "Got it?"

Eagle jolted awake. "Whah?"

"Dixon will be like Patton. He will create the diversion in the Orange Foods department. While he's doing that Eagle will be in charge of surveillance, and I will liberate the prisoners. We will then walk casually out the door in one-minute intervals."

Dixon was fired up. "I'm gonna be jutht like a thuper-hero. Like Aqua Man!" He pumped his fist in the air.

"Okay," Ti said. "Let's move out."

In the security office, a small, wiry, middle-aged guard named Sean, his hair buzzed to a gray stubble, was drinking his 16th Red Bull of the day and staring at one of the screens on the wall in front of him.

"What the hell is that?" he said to himself, his left eye twitching. He saw a little kid who looked like he might be in second grade, walking around the Fructose Department. The kid was wearing an adult's tan trench-coat that was so big on him about a third of it dragged behind him on the floor. On his head he wore a man's brown fedora, covered with clear plastic, that came down below his ears, and huge, gold-trimmed sunglasses reminiscent of Elvis in his fat period. The kid kept looking around suspiciously.

Near him was another kid, a few years older, wearing baggy jeans, gold-painted basketball shoes, a tank-top undershirt, and bling. This kid was also swiveling his head around like a paranoid periscope. They were up to something.

Suddenly a siren sounded on one of the monitors in Sean's office. In the Orange Foods Department, one of the Retail Advisors had apparently tripped her alarm button. Sean zoomed out the camera and saw a huge kid wearing a too-small black Batman t-shirt and torn pants. He was lying on his back in the Cheze Puffz aisle, his mouth open. Sean turned up the microphones for that department. He could hear the kid screaming, "Ow, my heart! I think it's broken! I think the mono and diglycerides in the orange food is giving me a heart invasion!"

Sean's other eye began to twitch. He could see the Retail Advisor in her orange smock leaning over the boy, who was clutching at his chest. He zoomed in the camera. Problem was, the kid who was claiming to have something wrong with his heart was grabbing the right side of his chest, not the side with an actual heart on it.

He looked back at the hip-hop punk and the midget kid, who were still glancing around nervously in the Fructose Department. Sure enough, the midget kid reached out, grabbed five jumbo Sugar Booms, and stuffed them into the pocket of his trench coat. Then he and the white gangsta headed straight for the exit doors like a couple of speed walkers. Meanwhile, back in the Cheze Puffz aisle, the blimp kid had miraculously recovered from his heart attack the second another Retail Advisor showed up with the special heart shockers, and he was now speed-walking out the exit, too.

Sean swiveled in his chair to look at the wall of monitors for the exterior cameras. The midget was taking off his trench coat while Heart Attack and Gangsta did chest bumps. Then the midget fished out three of the Sugar Booms from his coat and handed two of them to the other two criminals. They ripped off the paper and shoved them into their mouths like they hadn't eaten in days.

"Bunch a amateurs," Sean muttered.

With the flick of a switch Sean could have done what he usually did to shoplifters. He could have dropped the nets, raised the gates, and launched automatic gas bombs that would have sprayed them blue and knocked them out until the cops came.

Instead he just leaned back in his chair and cracked open another can of Red Bull.

Chapter Nine

"Them are *good*."

Johnny Fitziguzzi was lying on top of his bed wearing a powder-blue Snuggie. It and his face were covered with bits of powdered sugar and caramel. He smiled dreamily, like he was drunk. The brothers had just sold him the two remaining Sugar Booms, for which he'd given them three sweaty quarters, two sticky dimes, and five pennies that seemed to have peanut butter on them. The candy bars were the size of bricks, made of marshmallow with a caramel center, coated in cotton candy and a hard candy shell that was frosted, covered with sprinkles, glazed, and dusted with powdered sugar.

"So you did it, you kids," Johnny yelled over the sound of the TV, which was blasting a cartoon episode of "Flora the Explora" at top volume. "You pulled off your first job. You're real criminals now. How'd you like it?"

"It wath fun," Dixon said. "And we were tho, tho good at it."

"I think we've finally found our calling, Mister Fitziguzzi," Ti said politely, "Just like you said. We're freedom fighters. True banditos!"

"Yeah, Brah, it was da bomb," Eagle said.

"Sugar Boom?" Johnny tore the wrapper off the second enormous candy bar and took a bite.

"You sure that's a good idea?" his roommate Doc yelled.

"Sure it's a good idea," Johnny bellowed back at him, his mouth already stuffed with candy. "This's made wi' real cane sugar, so ith health food." He stuffed more of the bar into his mouth and chomped away. In seconds it was gone. A small stream of brownish drool trickled out of the side of his mouth and down his chin.

He began to quiver, starting with his head, then his mouth, his arms, his legs. His eyes got big. He jumped up on the bed and began bouncing like a toddler. "Weeeee!" he cried. He flapped his arms and jumped. His head bumped the ceiling. He rolled off the bed and ran back and forth in the tiny space between his bed and the door. He grabbed Ticonderoga by the hands and twirled him around like a dance partner.

Then, just as suddenly, he fell onto the bed, curled up, and stopped moving.

They looked at him for a while. Dixon shook his shoulder and yelled in his ear over the noise of the cartoon, "Mister Fitziguzzi? Are you dead?"

Johnny's arm flopped up and smacked Dixon in the face. He rolled onto his other side. Even over the television you could hear him snoring.

"You won't have to listen to any more of his horse manure for a couple of days now," Doc yelled from his bed. "He's got a sugar hangover. He's gonna have to sleep it off."

The three brothers stood there, unsure what to do.

"So get out of here," Doc yelled. "Go play in traffic."

"We did that yeth-terday," Dixon yelled back.

"Yeah," Eagle said. "It was fun."

"Now what?" Ti asked his brothers.

They were sitting in the bus shelter in front of the nursing home, one of their favorite hang-outs. It was the only shady spot in this part of town now that the trees had been sold, and the roof didn't leak, and since the buses barely ran anymore they usually had it all to themselves, aside from Jojo the Hobo, a former magazine executive who lived there.

"Whataya mean 'what do we do,' Brah? We go boost more Sugar Booms and pocket the green!"

"Think about it, Eagle," Ti said. "We need to get Castelli another 61 bucks by Friday or she beats the snot out of us."

"I'd kinda like that, I think," Dixon said. "She's got thuch fiery eyes."

"So we just need to boost another 122 Sugar Booms, yo!"

"It won't work," Ti said. "Two Sugar Booms and Johnny's asleep for two days. 122 would take four months, and it might kill him. And I'm not sure he *has* 61 bucks."

"I had 61 bucks once," said Jojo the Hobo from the corner of the bus shelter. He was a formerly handsome man in a formerly expensive suit who kept all his possessions in what was once a fancy leather briefcase. He spent a lot of his time talking on his cell-phone to famous people and advertisers, even though everyone knew his cell-phone no longer worked because he couldn't pay for service or batteries. "I had 61 thousand in cash I kept in the office safe just in case I needed to buy a car or get a model a new wardrobe."

"Shut up, Jojo," Eagle said. "We working our gangsta thing here."

"Fine," Jojo said, sounding hurt. "But don't come to me when you want to be on the cover of my magazine."

"Your magazine is toast, Brah," Eagle said. "It's a website now. They run it in India. Everybody knows that."

"I could go for toast right now," Dixon said. "Maybe a whole-grain thour dough? With butter on it?"

"Guys," Ti said. "We've got to find a way to pay Castelli."

"She hath a tattoo on her arm!"

"Yo, Brah," Eagle said, smacking Ti on the shoulder. "Try to look on the bright side here. We found our calling. We be real gangstahs now. We knows how to boost stuff. So let's boost something that's worth a big stack of dead presidents. Like a case of forties maybe. Or a nine-millimeter. Or a phone."

"If I wath gonna go shopping right now," Dixon said, "I'd get the new Batman movie on DVD and an All-Clad thauté-pan. It'th hard to braise a thquirrel properly in that cast-iron thing I have to use."

"I worked at *Gourmet* you know," Jojo said. "The make-your-own-yogurt craze? I started that."

"Jojo, if you don't quit your buggin' I'm gonna slap you." Eagle turned back to his brothers. "We boost something big," he continued, "we fence it, then we can pay off Castelli and still have enough Benjamins left over to hire some hot dancers for my video."

"But who would we sell them to?"

"All my rich homeys over to Brimmingham."

"That's brilliant," Ti said.

"'Course it is, yo. I always be brilliant."

"I was brilliant once," Jojo said. "You know those cards that fall out of magazines? I invented those."

"You know what, Jojo?" Ti said. "You should be ashamed of yourself."

Chapter Ten

"Do we have to use the tunnel?" Ti whined. "It's so dark!"

They were standing in a corner of the overgrown lot near their bus. Eagle had moved aside an old, rusty washing machine to reveal a hole in the ground lined with cardboard, cinderblocks, and scraps of plywood.

"Yeah, Brah," Eagle said gently.

"And it's dirty," Ti said. He pointed to his t-shirt, onto which he'd drawn lapels, buttons, and pockets. "This is my best suit."

"I don't think I can fit through there," Dixon said.

"Can't we just go through the Welcome Center?" Ti asked.

"No way, Brah," Eagle said. "To get to the Welcome Center you got to get into the town, and they won't let you through the town gate without an official stamped invitation from someone who lives there. Trust me, homey, I've tried."

Brimmingham Academy may have been just a few hundred feet from their bus, but it was in a different world. They could practically throw an empty bottle from the weeds in their lot to the lush grass of this exclusive boarding school, but it was across the border in the much wealthier town of North Southington. The town had a high cast-iron fence around it with gilded points and stone gates manned by security guards.

Eagle, however, had long since dug a tunnel down through the packed yellow clay on their side, under the gate, and into the rich dark loam of Brimmingham.

He had done this because every spring, after the limousines came to take the students back to their first homes in Greenwich or their second and third homes in Milan and Bermuda, servants removed all the things that had been left behind in the dormitories and piled them up in one of the covered plazas for removal to the landfill. Eagle had gotten several years' worth of clothes from this pile, often still in its new, original packaging, as well as unused phones, computers, and lacrosse sticks, which he would bring home, sell, and use the money to buy food.

He had also made friends with many of the students, who thought he was a curiosity. "Dude!" Apley Court Wigglesworth had said, pointing to Eagle, when he had first introduced him to Parker Worthington, another Brimmingham student. "This dude's, like, never been helicopter skiing! And he only has, like, one house."

"It ain't even a house, Brah," Eagle had said proudly. "It's a bus." Most of the students at Brimmingham, who had never seen actual slums or ghetto dwellers, thought Eagle was a real gangsta, and he liked that.

Eagle had also mastered two skills the kids at Brimmingham considered useful. He could pick locks, which came in handy when one of them had had a favorite Rolex or golf club confiscated by a teacher. He also knew how to hack into the school's computer system. Thanks to Eagle, Taran Rata, the son of a Bangladeshi billionaire, had just been accepted to Harvard. It probably didn't matter, since Rata's father had just funded a $26.2-million building at the Harvard Business School, but Eagle had changed all of the Ds on Rata's record to Bs, and changed all the reports in his file about "binge drinking" to "binge giving." As a thank-you, Rata had given him a case of champagne. "Here," he'd said. "Take this. It isn't even French."

But now his big brother was pacing nervously in front of the tunnel opening, rubbing his hands together and muttering to himself, "What would Thpidey do?"

"Dixon," Eagle said.

"Whaaa?" Dixon said. He seemed ready to cry.

"Did you know that over there at Brimmingham they have an omelet bar in the dining room open 24 hours a day, and you don't even have to pay, and they'll make it with whatever ingredients you want?"

"Like black-truffle mushrooms?" Dixon said excitedly. "And prosciutto ham?"

"Mos' def," Eagle said.

"Let'th go!" Dixon grabbed Ti's little wrist and jumped down into the hole. Eagle followed, pushing them both from behind. A minute or so later Dixon lifted a trap door Eagle had cut in the wooden floor of a barn and pulled himself up. He stood, looked around at the dusty lawnmowers, piles of tools, and bags of fertilizer, then pulled Ti up behind him.

When Eagle had joined them, Dixon said to him, "Is thith the dining room? Where'th the omelet bar? If you lied to me, Eagle, I'm gonna pinch you."

"Brah," Eagle said, "Chillax. This a garden shed, Brah. They store stuff here. And they barely even use it since they built that new one over there." He pointed through a dusty window to what looked like an enormous Victorian house across the perfect golf-course of a lawn with a large sign in front that read "The Simon and Sheila Wilfrank Memorial Landscape Maintenance Center."

"Act like you belong here," Eagle said. He adjusted his plastic bling, moved his flat hat a little more to the side, and opened up the door of the barn. The light that poured in was like nothing Ti had ever seen before: It was bright and clean and yellowy, like gold.

Out on the lawn, Dixon's mouth fell open. Ti had a slightly smug look, as if he was thinking that one day he would own all this. Before them they saw huge marble buildings with white columns and gilded lettering. The buildings were arranged around a central courtyard of thick grass, tall elm trees, statues of old men, tame antelope, and a burbling fountain coated with gold. The air smelled of roses, lilacs, and grilling steaks.

Groups of students walked along the brick pathways. The girls wore burgundy blazers, striped ties, and short green skirts. The boys wore the same blazers and ties with green shorts. One girl with blonde hair twirled some kind of tiny tennis racquet and said to her friend, "Last weekend, when I was in like, D.C.? I was like, chillin' with my broker, and he was like, Yeah!"

"Is she a dummy or thomething?" Dixon asked.

The girl heard him, looked over, and gave him a look, as if he was circus freak.

"Chill, Brah," Eagle said. "Tha's how rich people talk."

Chapter 11

Ti and Dixon followed Eagle towards the far corner of the courtyard and up dozens of marble steps into an enormous building. A carved granite sign identified it as the Trump, Trump, & Trump Center for Residential Living.

"What is this place?" Ti whispered to Eagle. "Is it a church?"

"Ith it the White House?" Dixon asked.

"No way, Brah," Eagle said. "This be where rich kids sleep."

"They don't thleep in busses?"

"Only when they're tourin', Brah," Eagle said. "But their tour busses actually move."

Eagle approached the security guard, a muscled young guy with a dark tan who sat in the foyer of the dorm behind a fancy desk. "Yo, Tony!" Eagle said. "I gots to take an order from Parker." He hooked at thumb over his shoulder to his brothers. "These are my homeys."

They fist-bumped. "Hey, Eagle," Tony said. "How's it goin' man? Parker ain't here right now. He's down at the Polo Grounds. Didn't he tell you? He's playin' Position Number Three!"

"Ith that good?" Dixon asked.

"It's actually considered to be the most important position of the four," Ti said.

Eagle looked down at him. "Yo, Brah, is there anything you don't know?"

They walked across the courtyard to the far end, where a set of white marble steps led down to a vast sporting complex with green fields, tracks, and viewing stands. They found the polo match in front of the Cartier Ballon Bleu Watch Now Available in 18-Karat Gold Equestrian Center, but it appeared to be half-time. Eagle pointed out his friend Parker, who was sitting under a yellow-striped tent sipping an ice tea. They could see servants in knickers in front of the stables, combing and massaging the horses.

"Them horsies be tight, Yo," Eagle said.

"Are they eating huckleberry thcones?" Dixon asked.

"What, the horsies?"

"No, thilly! The rich folkth!" He pointed to where Parker was seated, surrounded by well-dressed, healthy looking people who were eating little sandwiches and pastries from three-tiered silver trays.

As they got closer Parker saw them and waved them over. He had dirty-blonde hair, combed back and held in place with gel, and a smug expression. "Francesca," he said to a bird-faced girl with long brown hair who was seated next to him, "this is Eagle. He's like, poor."

Francesca didn't say anything, but she almost smiled.

"Yo, Homey," Eagle said, and gave Parker a fist-bump. "How my best prepster?"

"Smashing! We're up five to nil after the first chukker."

Eagle looked confused, but he smiled and said, "That's snorky."

"So Eagle," Parker asked him, flicking two fingers at Dixon and Ti. "Who are those people? Are they also, you know, poor?"

Ti stepped up and shook Parker's hand briskly. "Hello, sir," he said. "My name is Ticonderoga. I'm Eagle's brother. This is our oldest brother, Dixon. It's a pleasure to meet you."

"Gracious," Parker said, smiling at Eagle. "The little man is smooth. Is he a future politician perhaps?"

"No," Ti said, "I'm actually the head of a criminal enterprise. We're the Pencil Bandits."

"Excellent!" Parker said. "My uncle's a criminal."

"Really," Ti said. "What line of crime is he in?"

"I'm not entirely sure," Parker said, and took a sip of iced tea. "He did an insider trading of some sort. We no longer talk."

"Ith he in jail?" Dixon asked.

Parker chuckled, as if the question was incredibly stupid. "Of course not! He has *lawyers!*"

Over in the stands, a servant in red velvet knickers blew on a polished hunting horn.

"Sorry fellows," Parker said, "but the next chukker is starting. No more time to party."

"We ain't here to party, Brah," Eagle said. "We here to do business. We wanna boost you some stuff."

"Boost?"

"You know. Shop lift."

"Shop lift?"

"Yeah, Brah. Whataya need. The new iPad 17?"

"I've already got two," Parker said. "Or maybe three. I just bought another one in red, because it matched my Hermes bathrobe."

"Cell phone?"

"I've got like, six."

"A blender?" said Dixon.

"Funny!" said Parker. "Isn't that one of those machines that waiters use to make my smoothies?"

"Parker!" A very serious-looking grown-up in a blue blazer and white pants was yelling from the sidelines of the polo field. "It's time to take your mount!"

Parker stood up, drained the ice tea, fist-bumped with Eagle, and waved two fingers at Ti and Dixon. "Duty calls!" He wandered off towards the stables.

The brothers stood there for a few minutes, eyeing the remaining tray of little sandwiches and pastries on the table, wishing they could grab them. Then they noticed that the bird-faced girl was staring at them as if they were a type of animal at the zoo she'd never seen before.

Ti tapped his brothers on their shoulders, smiled to Francesca, bowed slightly, and said, "We'll go now."

Eight young riders on eight ponies galloped onto the field. Eagle said, "Pretty horsies. I want a horsie."

"Some day," Ti said, patting him on his back. "Some day."

A few minutes later they had climbed the marble stairs and were walking across campus, arguing loudly. "But I want an omelet," Dixon was saying. "You promithed me a omelet!"

"No," Ti was saying. "We've got work to do."

"But I'm hungry, thilly!" Dixon said. "I really need thome prosciutto! You thaid I could have an omelet with black truffles and prosciutto, and I'm not going back into that icky tunnel 'til I get one!"

They were so deep in conversation that they hadn't noticed the person following them. Until the siren went off.

The three brothers jumped. Behind them they saw a man who must have weighed 300 pounds in a white police-style uniform and safari helmet, standing on a Segway, a blue light spinning on its top. He flicked off the siren and stared at them, as if they'd done something horribly wrong.

Ti counted the man's chins. He stopped counting after three. Ti smiled and said, "Can I help you, Officer?"

"You boys are out of uniform," the man said. He pulled a narrow pad from a hatch on the Segway. "Lemme see your IDs. I'm gonna have to write you up for this."

"What'th gonna happen?" Dixon said. "Am I gonna get my omelet?"

"I don't know anything about an omelet, young man," the officer said, very serious. "You'll have to take that up with the Director of Food Services." He gestured towards a building about fifty yards behind them.

Dixon turned and saw what looked like an enormous castle. At the top of its stone steps he could see a sign that read "Norman and Melinda Bates Memorial Center for Nutritional Dining." His eyes got big.

"You know the fine for being out of uniform," the security guard was saying, filling in boxes on a ticket form. "Five hundred dollars each, assuming it's your first offense."

"But officer," Ti said, giving him his biggest, most charming smile, the smile that was so good it made the ticket-taker at the movie theater believe him every time he said he'd left his ticket stub inside the theater. "We're out of uniform because we're in the school play."

"Yeah yeah," the guard said. "You think I haven't heard that one before? Lemme see your IDs, before I call your parents."

"We don't got 'em on uth," Dixon said, looking unusually clever.

"Why not?"

"They're in our backpackth."

"Oh really?" said the guard. "Then where are your backpacks?"

"They're over there!" Dixon said, pointing at the dining castle. "Right next to the omelets!"

The guard said, "I'll escort you."

Dixon slapped his brothers and yelled, "Run!"

He took off towards the castle at a speed neither of his brothers realized he possessed. They had no choice but to follow.

The security guard clicked on his Segway's siren, leaned forward, and took off after them. He had just about caught up to them when they reached the castle's steps. The three brothers ran up them, two at a time. The guard gunned his Segway onward, but the front tires just bumped into the stone. He backed up, drove forward faster at the steps, hit them, and fell over.

By the time the guard had gotten back up on his feet the brothers were sixteen steps up, about halfway to the door. The guard abandoned his Segway and climbed up the first step, then the second. Then he stopped to catch his breath. By now the brothers had gained another ten steps on him. He took two more steps, then stopped again, panting.

By the time the guard abandoned the chase on step seven and stopped to clutch his chest, Dixon had already ordered his black-truffle and prosciutto omelet.

Chapter 12

The Faber brothers had never seen so much food in their lives.

The Norman and Melinda Bates Memorial Center for Nutritional Dining seemed to be about the size of a football field. White marble columns supported a gilded ceiling painted with angels and clouds that surrounded skylights of green glass. The walls were covered with dark-wood panels and paintings of old white people in golden frames. Beside the tall windows hung golden curtains rumored to contain actual hair from the heads of George Washington, Thomas Jefferson, and Warren G. Harding. In the balcony, a quartet of musicians played Schubert and Bach.

Students sat in golden chairs at tables covered with white clothes, attended by servants wearing gloves, velvet knickers, and tunics. On a long line of cloth-covered tables, monitored by still more gloved and uniformed servants, they could see shiny silver pans piled high with steaming, deliciously fragrant food. Some of the servants were carving slices from what looked like the entire legs of beef and ham, others were blending wheat-grass and carrot juice into smoothies, others were spooning caviar onto freshly made crepes.

"What do we do now?" Ti whispered to his brothers. He had directed them off to a corner behind some columns, where he'd hoped they couldn't be seen, and was feeling nervous about getting caught.

"Would you care to help yourself to the buffet?" said a voice behind them.

They turned to see an elderly man with a mustache in a velvet suit, bowing slightly.

"Or," he said, "Would you prefer to order from the menu?"

"Both!" Dixon said.

They sat at a table and ordered beverages from the menu: a pitcher of freshly squeezed orange juice, three cappuccinos, and a large bottle of Evian sparkling mineral water.

While Dixon bee-lined toward the omelet station, Eagle, who preferred orange foods, stepped up to the buffet line, where he selected candied yams, turkey bacon covered in hollandaise sauce, and six fried eggs, from which he requested that the white parts be removed. Ti ordered a bowl of chocolate Cheerios, four pieces of wheat toast covered with raspberry preserves, and a jelly doughnut.

While his brothers leaned back in their chairs, stomachs bulging, Dixon had a second omelet, this time filled with foie gras and Camenbert. Then he got a plate of Belgian waffles covered with strawberries and cream. He was just sawing into a rare porterhouse steak covered in pork chops when they heard a panting noise. Behind them, an out-of-breath voice said, "I've *got* you!"

They looked.

It was the security guard with the multiple chins.

Eagle said, "Yo, it's about time, Brah! We been in here chowin' for like, an *hour*!"

Ti said, "Run!"

"Not now!" Dixon wailed. "I gotta finish my pork chopth!"

Ti grabbed two off his plate and sprinted towards the back of the dining center.

Dixon ran after him yelling, "Hey! Gimme those back!"

They ran through a pair of high, mahogany doors into a long hallway. The walls were made of dark-wood paneling covered with more oil portraits of old white people.

In one corner, a tall girl in the school uniform with long, strawberry-blonde hair was threatening a waiter with her lacrosse stick. "Bad, Wesley! That's the second time this semester you've served me over-cooked eggs."

"Hey, foxy!" Eagle said to her.

She looked at him with contempt. "What?"

Ti grabbed Eagle's arm and pulled him towards the far end of the hallway toward another pair of high, mahogany doors.

They found themselves in yet another hallway, similar to the previous one except that these walls were covered with tooled leather. Two boys in school uniforms who looked like they were in kindergarten were hitting golf-balls on the long oriental carpet with short clubs.

"Is that a birdy?" a boy with wavy hair was saying to a short kid with ketchup on his forehead.

The Faber brothers jumped over the golf balls, ran to the end of that hallway, and pushed through another set of high, mahogany doors. They stopped, confused: Somehow they were now back into the first hallway, where the strawberry blonde leaned on her lacrosse stick wagging her finger at the waiter, who was on his knees, weeping. At the far end of the hallway, the doors that came from the dining center burst open. Ti yelped when he saw the multi-chinned security guard struggling through, his white pith helmet ajar.

"Aha!" the guard yelled. "I've got you!"

Ti turned his brothers around and led them back into the hallway where the kindergarteners were putting.

"Par three?" said the boy with the ketchup on his forehead.

"Quick!" Ti said. "In here!"

He herded his brothers through a side door and pushed it shut. The three of them leaned against the inside of the door, trying to keep it closed. They could hear the big mahogany doors swing open, then heavy footsteps. The children stopped their chattering about golf and said to someone, "Are you all right, officer?"

"I'm fine," they could hear the guard puff.

"Should we call Medical Services?"

"Why?"

"Because your face is clammy, you're short of breath, and you're holding your chest? And my mother says those are common signs of a heart attack?"

They heard a loud thud. It sounded as if something heavy had hit the wall and was sliding down it.

"Now should we call Medical Services?" said a little voice.

"Yes!" barked the guard.

Ti cracked the door open a quarter inch and looked out. He could see the guard slumped against the wall, his face yellow. The kindergartener with the ketchup on his head had a tiny cell-phone in his hand and was poking numbers.

"Poop!" Ti whispered to his brothers.

"What?"

"That guard is dying out there. We'll be stuck in here for hours, until they can cart him away."

"What ith thith place?" Dixon said. He was looking around. It was big and bright, the walls and floor covered with white, shiny tile. Behind them it opened up into the cleanest, brightest, whitest room they'd ever seen, with chandeliers and mirrors on the far wall. It smelled like lavender and roses and spring rain.

"I think it's an operating room," Ti said.

"Nah, homeys," Eagle said. "You were right about the poop. This be where the Brimminghams go to the baffroom!"

"Really?" Dixon said. "I wanna live here."

"Me too," said Ti.

"But it's a bathroom for *women*," said a female voice.

A tall, beautiful girl with short black hair, her skin the same color as the cappuccino they'd just enjoyed in the dining center, had appeared from around the corner. She was standing in front of them, her arms crossed.

""What are you doing here?" she demanded. "Do I have to call Security?"

Dixon said, "I think Thecurity jutht died."

Chapter 13

Two more girls joined the first one. One was short and freckled, the other brown-haired and frighteningly thin. It seemed as though they had just smeared their faces with chocolate sauce.

"Wait a thecond," Dixon said. "Ith that chocolate thauce?"

The girls looked at each other nervously. The short one dabbed at her face with her finger, licked it, and said, "Maybe."

"But we're not *eating* it," the thin one said contemptuously.

"Well then what do you be doin', girlfriend?"

"None of your business," the freckled one said.

"I'm not your *girlfriend*," said the thin one.

By now Ti had slipped behind them and checked out the larger room. It was big and beautiful, with fancy doors along one wall leading into what must have been toilet stalls, and another wall of sinks. One of the sinks was surrounded by a brown mess. He poked his finger in a soup bowl by the sink.

Ti said, "Chocolate sauce!"

"Yo yo yo," Eagle said, amused. "Why you crazy brizzles be puttin' chocolate on your fizzles?"

"Call security," the freckled one said to the tall one.

"Yeah," Ti said. "They're definitely going to want to get some pictures of *this*."

"Pictures?" The thin one shrieked a little and clattered away on her high heels. They heard one of the doors of the stalls slam shut, then paper towels being furiously pulled from a dispenser.

"Wait a second," said the tall girl to Eagle. "Don't I know you?"

Eagle leered up at her. "Not as much as I'd like to know you, Breezy!"

"I do know you," the girl said, and smiled. "You're that friend of Parker's, aren't you? You're the guy who's *poor*!"

"Tha's me, my sistah!" Eagle gave her a high-five.

The girl introduced herself. Her name was Brieahnaugh. (She spelled it for them.)

"You can like, *fix* stuff, right?" Brieahnaugh said. "On the computer? Like grades?"

The freckled one brightened. "Can he change my squash grade? I got a B."

"Mos' def, my sista! For the right amount of greens I can fix anything!"

"Wow," said the freckled girl. "I wish I was poor."

"But first," Ti said, eying the freckled girl warily, "you have to tell us what's up the chocolate sauce. Is this a religious thing?"

"No, no," Brieahnaugh said. "It's a beauty treatment. It's good for their skin." She gave him a coy look. "My skin doesn't need treatment."

"You got that right, girlfrien'," Eagle said. "You da bomb."

Brieahnaugh smiled.

"Doeth it work?" Dixon asked.

"Not with this crap," the very thin girl said. "Not enough cocoa solids, and no cocoa butter."

"It's much better with the truffles," the freckled girl agreed.

"But we can't get the truffles. We asked the head chef and everything. He said they're too unhealthy."

"Can you believe it?" the freckled girl said. "For what my dad pays in tuition, I could buy, like, a *house*. So we should get whatever we want."

"It's an outrage," Ti agreed. "You should sue." He was joking.

"We're working on it," Brieahnaugh said. "My mom is a lawyer for Phillip Morris. She says it's immoral."

"Yeah," Ti said, still joking. "Kinda like working for a company that sells cigarettes?"

"No, no," Brieahnaugh said. "Cigarettes create jobs!"

"Are we talking about black truffleth?" Dixon asked.

"Not exactly," Brieahnaugh said. "They're kinda brown."

"French?" Dixon asked.

"Swiss, I think," the thin girl said.

"The Thwiss don't grow a decent truffle," Dixon said.

"I think they do," said the freckled girl. "I think they're yummy."

"I like the ones with caramel inside," agreed Brieahnaugh.

"Thath criminal!" Dixon yelled so loudly that Ti shushed him.

Eagle, who hadn't been listening, perked up. "Was' criminal, homey? I'm in!"

"It'th criminal to take thomething as beautiful ath a black truffle and thtuff it with caramel! The flavorth are all wrong!" Dixon was so angry he looked frightening.

"Well all I know is," said Brieahnaugh, "they melt real well and make a beautiful facial mask that tones the skin and hides all signs of aging."

"Black truffleth?"

"Although I prefer the milk chocolate, not the caramel."

"Oh," said Dixon, and smiled. "*Chocolate* truffleth. That'th not criminal."

"So lemme get this straight, ma breezy little brizzles," Eagle said. "You lookin' for truffles made of chocolate so you can rub 'em on yo' face."

"Right!" said Brieahnaugh.

"Well you come to the right place, Sista! Me an' my homeys, we can set you up."

"Really?"

"Can you get us Lindt white-chocolate truffles?" the thin girl asked, eyeing him suspiciously.

"Yo, yo," Eagle said. "Fo' shizzle! If you gots the Benjamins."

"Huh?"

"He means you have to pay for them," Ti explained.

The freckled girl asked, "With money?"

"With money."

"Do you take credit cards?"

"No I don't take no credit cards, Bird!" Eagle said. "What do I look like, a Kmart?"

"What's that?"

"Never mind. I needs the green, sista! The pictures of the presidents! The big heads! The cash!"

Brieahnaugh said, "Well all I've got is like a hundred."

"That'll work."

"If I give you a hundred dollars can you get us like, ten?"

"Of what?"

"Those Lindt white-chocolate truffles. They're like, the size of golf ball."

"Sure!" Eagle turned to Ti and whispered, "Can we?"

"Yes!" Ti whispered back. "I saw them at Wally World!"

"Aha." Eagle turned towards the girls, smiled, and slapped Brieahnaugh's palm. "You gots a deal, Sista! How's about we make the pass tamarra?"

"Okay!" Brieahnaugh giggled, fished around in her purse, and handed him a hundred-dollar bill. They slapped palms, then fists, then shoulders, but she backed away when Eagle tried to give her a hug.

As the Faber brothers were walking across campus towards the underground tunnel and home they heard a siren behind them. Again. And it was getting closer.

"Are we guilty of murder?" Dixon whined.

"That guy's not dead," Ti assured him. "Remember? I saw them take him away on a stretcher."

"Yeah, but what if he died after that?"

"You there!" came a voice over a bullhorn. "You poor kids! Stop where you are!"

They didn't obey the voice, however. They ran.

Chapter 14

The bus-ride home from Burr Oak Elementary the following Monday was not as long as usual. Forty-three kids were still home sick with food poisoning from the Friday tacos, so the driver didn't have to make as many stops. Plus, the bus only broke down once.

Burr Oak Elementary students had once ridden to and from school in a fleet of six yellow busses. Since the tax cuts, however, it was now down to one tired, rusty old bus with pieces of plywood where some of the windows used to be. Most days it left school with 138 kids. They had to sit piled up on top of each other, in the aisles, and under the seats. Two kindergarteners had to sit on the seat with the driver, who was a very nice woman, but they complained that she smelled like motor oil. That's because besides driving the bus, the driver had to repair it: changing tires on the side of the road, tying together broken parts from her stash of coat hangers, or cleaning dirt from the clogged fuel lines. On a typical day the bus could take three hours to get the Faber brothers home, and they were far from the last ones to get off. Today it took less than two.

Ti, Eagle, and Dixon all took the same bus because they were all in the same class. Ti had skipped forward three grades, and Dixon had been kept back two. Dixon was actually quite brilliant, but he had dyslexia, which made it hard for him to read, and there were no longer any aids at Burr Oak to help.

Once inside their own bus—the one they lived in—they dumped their backpacks in a corner and patted their father on the head. He had worked two days the previous week, but was home sick again. Dixon made a little fire in the stove to boil water. They fixed their father a mason jar of tea made with sweet fern and medicinal herbs Dixon had collected near the swamp. It seemed to make him feel better.

Once their father was settled back onto his mattress and comfortably snoozing, Eagle took the crisp hundred-dollar bill they'd earned the day before from his hiding place and spread it out on the plywood board they used for a table. "Check out my big dog Benjamin here, homeys!"

They admired it for a bit.

"Okay," Eagle said at last. "Now I'ma go buy me some kickin' bling-bling!"

"Wait!" Ti said, but he was too late. Eagle had already run out the door and down the road.

When Dixon and Ti found him in the parking lot outside Wally World, they could tell that Eagle had already bought himself something because he was happily clutching the store's signature orange-plastic bag, the same bag you could see in gutters, ditches, and trees all over East Westford.

"Check it, check it!" Eagle said. He was sitting on the curb by the shopping-cart corral. He pulled something out of the bag and held it up for them to admire.

"What ith it?" Dixon asked.

"That's hideous," said Ti.

"What is it? What *is* it? Just the most def, the most doped up, the most down blingedy-bling you ever saw, Dawgs!"

He held up a rectangle of white metal, covered with sparkly rhinestones. In its center, blue LED lights flashed words that didn't make sense: "Im A Kool."

"What *ith* it?" Dixon repeated.

"It's a belt buckle, Boo. Ain't it kickin'? It's all iced out— with real *diamonds*!"

"I think those are plastic," Ti said. "And you don't own a belt."

Dixon studied it more closely. "What doeth 'Im a kool' mean?"

"It's Chinese," Ti said, "for 'I'm an idiot.'"

"Idiot?" Eagle said, indignant. "Who you callin' idiot, Fool? I got this on sale! It was only $44.95!"

"Huh," Dixon said. "Do you think maybe it wath on thale because it doethn't make any thenthe?"

Ti rushed Eagle and let loose a frenzy of slapping. Both hands flying, he smacked Eagle's chest, arms, cheeks, eyes, legs, and anything else he could reach. Ti was three-quarters his size, but Eagle curled his arms and legs around his face, trying to protect himself.

Finally Ti let out a scream so high and angry that a family of raccoons the size of Labrador Retrievers that lived by the dumpsters stopped eating garbage, looked up scared, and ran away. A very skinny man with only two lower teeth, one of the scores of people who lived in their cars on the edge of the parking lot, called over to him, "You okay, little guy? You want I should get my stick?"

"I'm okay." Ti waved to him and calmed himself down.

"Yo, Dawg," Eagle said, smoothing out his hoody and readjusting his flat-cap just the way he liked it, tilted and to the side. "What was that all about?"

"We needed that money!" Ti said. "That was our money!"

"*My* Benjamin," Eagle corrected him.

"*Our* money!"

"Hey, the bird give it to *me*."

"We're a family," Ti said, hard and cold. "We work together."

"He'th right," Dixon said. "We're a team, like the X-Men or the Avengers. Thith ith everybody's caper."

"And we needed that money," Ti continued, "to pay off Castelli."

"Cathtelli," Dixon said dreamily. "She hath pretty handth."

"Yeah, and two very hard nunchuks," Ti said, "Which she looked like she would very much enjoy using to crack open our skulls. You're taking that piece of junk *back*."

"Yeah," Dixon said. "Take it back."

"Too late, Boo," Eagle said.

"No it's not!" Ti insisted.

"Yeah it is," Eagle said.

"Why?" Dixon said.

"'Cause I already broke it," Eagle said, trying to smile. He held up the buckle, which now flashed, "Im   ool."

"Yeah you are," Ti said.

"Chillax, Brah," Eagle said. "We still got 65 dollars in change. That's more than enough to pay off Castelli."

"I like her thneakers, too," Dixon said. "They're red!"

"If it cost 45," Ti corrected him, "we've got 55 left. Not enough. And we could have *paid* for the truffles."

"No biggy, Dawg! So we boost a couple extra. You gotta learn to stop buggin' and start coolin'. C'mon. Let's dip." He motioned for them to follow him, and they did.

As they were walking towards the Wally World doors, one of the hobos that lived behind the Garden Center approached Eagle and pointed to the orange plastic shopping bag he was carrying. The hobo was wearing a tweed sport-coat, now wrinkled and dirty. Dixon recognized him: it was Mister Franklin, who'd been his fourth-grade teacher three times, until Mister Franklin had been laid off during another round of budget cuts.

"Hi, Mithter Franklin!" Dixon said.

"Hey, Dixon," the man said, and tried to smile. "Still drawing?"

"Thtill drawing," Dixon said.

"Still in fourth grade?"

"Nope!" Dixon said proudly. "Now I'm in fifth!"

"That's great," Mr. Franklin said. "That's really great."

"It ith great!" Dixon said. "In fifth grade, the teacher hath a book!"

"Say, Dixon," Mr. Franklin said, "I was wondering if I could have that bag."

Dixon looked at the bag in Eagle's hand. They'd already discussed that they'd use it to hide the truffles they were about to steal. "Actually," Dixon said, "We kinda need it for thomething."

"No biggy," Mr Franklin said. "I'll ask someone else." He headed off towards a large couple in pajamas who were heading for their car. "See ya, Dixon. Keep drawing!"

"Thankth, Mithter Franklin," Dixon said, but he was still confused about the bag. "Thay Mithter Franklin," he called after his former teacher. "What do you need a bag for?"

Mister Franklin smiled sheepishly and said, "I need to go Number Two."

In the Security Office, Sean rubbed his hand over the gray stubble on top of his head and finished a Red Bull. He had noticed the midget, the monster, and the hiphop nitwit the second they passed through the full body scans. He had followed their progress through the store on the tracking cameras. He watched the big one, who was wearing a too-small Superman t-shirt, do a flop in the middle of the Frosted Twinkles aisle. Sean turned on the microphones and heard him screaming, "Help! Help! My kidneys are broken!"

This time, Sean noticed, the midget went to the Imported Foreign Gourmet Delites department, which was actually just one shelf in a corner by the mylar balloons that contained a few bottles of hot sauce from Mexico, some mustard from England, Polish pickles, and various kinds of Swiss candy. He was now stuffing little wrapped balls of chocolate into a Wally World bag.

Yet again the midget and the fake gangsta, Sean noticed, high-tailed it for the exits as soon as they were done, quickly followed by the moose kid, whose kidneys, apparently, had miraculously healed themselves. Yet again, when they were outside, the kids celebrated with fist-bumps and high fives, then stuffed their mouths with the stolen booty.

Yet again Sean chose not to hit the big, red button in the middle of his security console that would have raised the gates, dropped the nets, and sprayed the little criminals with blue dye and pepper spray. Instead he just shook his head, twitched, and cracked open a 28-ounce bottle of Blue Raspberry Monsta Energee Drink.

Chapter 15

The Faber brothers waited until dark to crawl through their tunnel into Brimmingham Academy, so as to avoid attention from the school's security. They crept along the sides of the buildings, hiding behind bushes and statues, and followed Eagle up the fire escape of the Trump, Trump, & Trump Center for Residential Living to the window outside Parker Worthington's apartment.

Dixon and Ti had never been to Parker's living quarters before, and what they saw through the windows made their mouths fall open. The first room in front of them was as big as their classroom at school, except that it had a green-marble fireplace at one end with logs burning, tufted leather sofas, oriental carpets, and a crystal chandelier. It didn't have a bed in it; apparently he slept somewhere else.

Eagle tapped the special code on the insulated glass—three longs, two shorts, three shorts, one long, an extended drum roll, a head bump, and three more longs. Before he was halfway through, Parker looked up from the corner, where he was sitting in an armchair smoking a pipe and staring at an iPhone. Parker smiled, got up—he was wearing a red-velvet bathrobe and duck slippers—and opened the window.

"Hullo, my poverty-stricken compadres!" Parker said. "Come in!"

Dixon noticed a big, shiny refrigerator in the kitchen and bee-lined for it. They could hear pans rattle and bacon sizzling.

"To what do I owe this privilege?" Parker asked. He waved towards a silver ice bucket and said, "Glass of champagne?"

"Yeah, Brah! Hook me up!"

"Not right now," Ti said, holding up his hand like he was stopping traffic. "We've got work to do."

"Work? How quaint."

"Oh yeah," Eagle said. "I forgot. Chillaxin' in the hood later, but right now we gotta find that breezy bird Brieahnaugh."

"Oh, Brieahnaugh," Parker said admiringly. "She is breath-taking. Do the four of you have a date?"

"Not exactly, Mang. We just here to make a delivery. Where she be at?"

"Typically," Parker said, "she spends a great deal of time after dinner enjoying the company of some other fine ladies in one of the spas at the Rec Center."

He explained how to get there, gave them one of his extra ID cards, and expressed the hope that they'd "pop in for a proper visit" later. "Some friends of mine and I will be watching the opening match in the World Series of Polo," he said. "I think you'll find it exhilarating."

"Oh fuh sure," Eagle said.

They found Dixon in the kitchen, where he had just finished pouring hollandaise on a bacon-and-egg sandwich. He stuffed the entire thing into his mouth and followed them towards the elevator.

When Parker had said "Rec Center," the brothers had imagined something like the East Westford YMCA, where they had gone a couple of times before a lack of paying members had forced it to close its doors. There had been an old flaking pool in the basement, a basketball court with several missing floorboards, and an exercise room occupied by a family of rabid opossums.

The William Howard Taft Center for Recreational Enrichment at Brimmingham Academy, however, was nothing like the Y. It was big and new, with frosted glass walls that rose many stories into the night sky. Using Parker's platinum pass-card, they were able to access it through a tunnel from the dormitory and ride an elevator from the basement to the first floor.

They walked down long corridors, off of which they saw many small rooms. Some of the little rooms contained green grass and giant TV screens of golf courses with nets in front of them, at which students were hitting golf balls with clubs. Other rooms looked like small white boxes, with wooden floors and lines painted on the walls. Most of them were empty, but in one of them two students in white shirts and shorts were hitting a ball off the walls with strange-looking tennis racquets.

"What ith that?" Dixon said.

Ti said, "ping pong." Actually it was a game they'd never seen before, called squash. None of the rooms, however, contained Brieahnaugh.

Another room, bigger than a football field, housed a rubbery oval track and a golf green, but that was empty aside from five workers in gray uniforms polishing the armrests in the viewing stands. They checked a room full of weight machines and what looked like torture devices. They checked all four pools on the next floor—the huge one, the hot one, the cold one, and the other huge one—but didn't see her. Finally they asked a janitor, who suggested they try the spa area on the eighth floor.

When they got off the elevator on the eighth floor they walked through a restaurant where students in gym clothes were sitting at mahogany tables, sipping fruit smoothies and cappuccinos while tapping on their phones. They wandered down a hallway, peering into the little, steamed up windows in the wooden doors. Inside they could see students sitting on wooden benches in their bathing suits, next to boxes of glowing red coals. They were sweating a lot, which they seemed to enjoy. Ti explained to his brothers that this was a special religious activity for rich people.

"Jam!" Eagle said. "When we be rich I'ma git me twelve a them, and six for Daddy."

Eventually they came to a tiled archway and entered another huge room which contained a shallow pool.

This pool took up much of the space, but it was so clean and still it looked like it had never been used. They could see a picture in its bottom made of tiny tiles that depicted a pretty young girl wearing nothing but her long, curling, golden hair, standing on a beach in a giant shell that Dixon identified as a scallop. Above the pool was a ceiling supported by fluted columns, and on the ceiling was another picture made from little tiles. This one depicted some old guy in a towel with a long, flowing white beard, reaching his finger out and touching the finger of a younger man who was completely naked.

Ti used the picture as an opportunity to lecture his older brothers about stranger danger. He had barely gotten through the part about men in big white vans offering candy when Eagle spotted three women and wandered over towards them. His brothers followed.

The women all wore white uniforms. They were leaning over three students lying on their stomachs on what looked like narrow beds, except that they were covered in soft white leather. The women in uniforms were poking and pushing at the students' bodies the way Dixon poked and pushed at his bread dough. The brothers knew what this was from watching "The Really Rich Housewives of Saudi Arabia" on Johnny Fitziguzi's television: the students were getting massaged.

When Eagle asked about Brieahnaugh and her friends—and Ti translated—one of the uniformed women said, "Oh, those three have already had their massages. Now they're over at the Mittney Bain Center for Pet Recreation, with their dogs." She explained how to get there.

The Mittney R. Bain Center for Pet Recreation was somewhat smaller than the Taft Center, but no less fancy. Inside the marble-tiled lobby, the Faber brothers faced a series of doors labeled with different types of pets: dogs, cats, horses, aquatics, reptiles, marsupials, endangered species, and teacup lions.

The brothers used Parker's card to buzz themselves through the dog door, and found themselves in another lobby, this one carpeted and paneled with dark wood and smelling of the cozy fire in the fireplace at one end. Eagle stood with his mouth open in wonder before a row of illuminated photographs on the walls. He explained that each one was a famous dog that had won a major competition. He pointed out details of their fancy costumes and spoke their names with hushed awe.

"This Pekingese is named Palace Garden Malarky," he said.

"Thounds like a Chinese Restaurant," Dixon said. "Mmmm, do you think they have Thai Thtyle lo mein?"

"And this," Eagle said, "is Roundtop BMW of Glasgow, a Scottish terrier."

"Mmmm," Dixon said. "haggis."

"And Good Times Spicey, a miniature poodle. Look at her cute little pompoms, Brah!"

"I like thpicey. I like Frank'th Hot Thauce. And jalapeños!"

At the end of the hall, two guards sat at a desk, monitoring who entered the only door. Dixon looked at them nervously—he was still worried about whether the guard with the multiple chins had died—but Ti had earlier grabbed a fancy silver shopping bag he found on a side chair and used it to store the truffles. Now he waltzed up to the guards like he owned the place, waved the bag, and said to them, "We're here to deliver the hair gel."

"Okay." The guard hit a button, the door buzzed open, and the three brothers walked through.

On the other side of that door, the Fabers found themselves in a gym for dogs. Except that it didn't smell like the YMCA; it smelled like the miniature rainforest they'd visited inside a greenhouse on a field trip to a local college, before the field trips had been discontinued due to budget cuts. They walked through groves of bamboo trees, blooming orchids, flower gardens, and sandy areas where the dogs could poop or pee on little fire hydrants. Attendants in white uniforms stood nearby with little rakes and shovels, ready to clean up.

Beyond the gardens the brothers could see work-out areas with dog treadmills, a swimming pool where the dogs wore special diapers, and a dog masseuse, all of it accompanied on hidden speakers by beautiful, dog-related music. Eagle said, "Is that Doggy Bounce, by the Crazy Dogggz? I love that tune. It's kareemy!"

He was also enthralled by the various dogs. "Look, mang!" he said to Dixon, who was far more interested in testing the real mangos he saw growing on a tree near the nail salon. "A German Panzer terrier. Them worth some serious coin. Ooooh, and I loves me that Kalahari Water Dog. And check out the Ultra-miniature Poodle!"

"It's smaller than a mouse," Ti said.

"Yeah," Dixon agreed with disgust. "Only good for about one bite."

Search as they might, however, the brothers couldn't find Brieahnaugh and her friends. Finally, after they'd walked by her three times, a friendly attendant who was wiping dog spit off what looked like a rowing machine asked if they needed help. When they admitted that they did and explained why, she pointed at a sign reading "Canine Smiles."

She said, "Room 13, on your left."

They found it and knocked. A woman's voice told them to come in. The room looked like pictures they'd seen in magazines of a doctor's office: white walls, tile floor, cabinets, lots of lights.

There was none of the screaming or crowds they were used to at the Emergency Room. A poster on the wall showed a dog lying back in some kind of a lounge chair with metal stuff on its teeth, and under it big bone-shaped letters reading, "You're A Doggone Good Patient!"

Brieahnaugh was with the same two friends they'd met in the bathroom of the dining center—the short, freckled one and the frighteningly skinny one. They were all dressed as if they were about to go out to a nightclub, in tight skirts, heels, earrings and make-up, and all three of them held one or two tiny dogs in her arms.

A fluffy little white dog with pink bows in its hair lay on its back in one of those reclining chair things. A woman in a white lab coat was doing something to its teeth. The girls didn't acknowledge the Faber brothers; they kept their attention focused on the dog in the chair.

"You're a good girl, Priscilla," the freckled one was saying. She held up the little dog in her hands to face the dog in the chair and said in baby-talk, "Tell her, Paris. Isn't Priscilla a good girl?"

Eventually Brieahnaugh did notice the Faber brothers. She smiled and said, "Oh, hi Eagle. Are you still, like, *poor*?"

"I'm so poor I eat food from dumpsters!" Eagle said.

Brieahnaugh laughed. "You are too funny!"

The freckled girl said to the skinny girl, "What's a dumpster?"

The skinny girl said, "It's a *restaurant*, but it's like, really, really cheap."

"These your dogs?!" Eagle asked, excited. He held his arms out to take the little spotted thing Brieahnaugh was holding.

She pulled it away in horror. "Yes," she said.

"How come you got six?"

"Our regular lap dogs, and our back-up dogs, stupid," the very thin one said.

"Why you need back-ups?"

"In case our starters get sick or something," Brieahnaugh said with a laugh. "Jeeze, don't they teach you poor kids anything?"

Eagle said, "Can I have one?"

"No!"

"Can I hold one?"

"No!"

Just then the skinny girl's dog, an obese, short-haired Chin named Tempura, jumped away from her and ran towards Dixon's sneaker, which still smelled like dead chipmunk. Eagle got down on his hands and knees, face to face with the pooch, and tried to pet it. The dog, smelling the remains of dinner on Eagle's face, licked his cheek.

"Stop it!" the thin girl barked at Eagle. "You'll get her tongue dirty."

"Sorry, Brizzle, but I gots a thing for dogs. I likes dogs way better than kids."

"Yeah," the skinny girl actually agreed. "A dog doesn't make you all fat and ruin your body, like having a kid does."

"Yeah," Brieahnaugh said. "An' a dog will never steal your credit cards and fly to Vegas, like my little sister did."

Eagle laughed. "Thas good, Sista!" He pointed to Dixon: "Draw that up!"

Brieahnaugh explained that five of the dogs were there to give moral support to Priscilla, the one lying in the chair. She said Priscilla was getting her braces adjusted.

Eagle said, "Doggy *braces*? What's that for?"

"Cross-bite, stupid."

"That's bad?"

"It is if you don't want your dog to get cavities."

"Do dogs get cavities?" Ti asked.

"They do if they don't get braces!" the freckled girl said.

Eagle said, "I wanna be your pet."

"You're not cute," the girl said.

While the doctor squirted Priscilla's teeth with compressed air and fitted a little circle of metal around one of its teeth, Brieahnaugh said, "What are you doing here?"

Eagle said, "We brought you that dank you ordered. Remembah?"

"Oh."

Ti handed her the bag and smiled.

The emaciated girl reached into the bag like a savage, grabbed a chocolate, unwrapped it, and began rubbing it over her cheeks. "Awesome!" she said. "I can feel my wrinkles fading already."

Ti had stolen a total of 23 white-chocolate truffles, but he and his brothers had eaten 11 of them, leaving the ten that the girls had already paid for, plus two extras. The girls agreed to Ti's suggestion that they buy the two extra truffles for an additional twenty dollars. This, however, created a problem.

"You *still* don't take like credit cards?" said the emaciated girl, as if she couldn't believe they were that incompetent.

"I could take it, ma sistah," Eagle grinned at her, "but I might not give it back!"

"Don't any of you ladies have cash?" Ti asked.

"What for?" said the freckled girl.

"Oh, you know," Dixon tried to explain. "You use it to buy thtuff, like arugula."

"Isn't that what credit cards are for?"

"I might have some more cash," Brieahnaugh said. "It's good for cleaning sunglasses." She pointed to a purse on the table behind Eagle. It was made of pink leather and covered with sparkling white stones that spelled the word "Chanel."

Eagle examined it as he handed it over. "Those are actual diamonds, ain't they, sista?"

"Yeah. I guess. Whatever."

"Can I have it?"

Brieahnaugh laughed and waved her hand at Eagle. "You're so funny. This old thing? It's last season." She opened the purse and fished around inside. "Score!" She held up a crumpled piece of green currency and handed it to Ti.

Ti opened up the ball of money and smoothed it out on his thigh. He said, "This is a hundred. We don't have change for this."

"Tha's cool, Brah," Eagle said. "Sista wants us to keep the change."

"No way!" the freckled girl said. "That's *hers*. You can't just come in here and take our money."

"Any smaller bills in your purse?" Ti asked.

"In this country the pieces of paper money are all the same size, stupid," said the emaciated girl.

"I meant smaller amounts," Ti said, flashing his most adorable smile. "Such as fifties or twenties."

"Oh."

Brieahnaugh said, "I'll check." She removed everything in her purse and laid it on a side table—three phones, a smaller pink leather bag also covered in diamonds that contained make-up, a thick stack of credit cards held together with a hair band, and a ham sandwich. Then she turned the purse upside down. She smiled at Ti and said, "That's all I got!"

"Yo, sista-woman," Eagle said. "How's about we just take the Benjamin and brings you the change in the a.m.?"

"No way!" the freckled girl said again. "You're poor! You'll just blow it all on cars and drugs!"

"Will not," Eagle said.

"Will too," said the freckled girl, sticking her chin out so it was practically touching his.

"Will not!"

"Will too!"

"Will *not*!" Eagle said. "You can't even buy a car for eighty dollars. They cost like, two hundred."

"Can too."

"Can not."

"Can too!"

"Can not!"

Ti stepped between them and held up his hands for them to stop. "I have an idea."

"What?" said the freckled girl.

"Maybe there's a store or restaurant on campus," he said. "A place that takes cash. They might be able to make change."

"There's the sushi bar!" the emaciated girl said, brightening. "Let's go there and like, order a whole bunch of really awesome sushi and smell it but not eat it!"

"It closed at ten," said the freckled girl.

"What about the phone store?"

"It closes at nine," said Brieahnaugh.

"The acupuncture store, in the basement of the Science building? I saw someone give them cash money once."

"Didn't you hear?" said the emaciated girl. "They got shut down yesterday for using sheets with a low thread-count."

"That sucks," Brieahnaugh said. "Hey. What about the book store?"

"You mean that dark place that sells the books?"

"Yeah," she said. "They're open 24 hours. They have to be because they sell pizza."

"C'mon then," Eagle said. "Let's get ghost."

The Ye Olde Literature Shoppe and Pizzeria at Brimmingham Academy looked more like a gift store at a historical theme park than a place that sold books. It was small, with a low, beamed ceiling, dark wooden walls, quaint, old-fashioned windows, and an overpowering smell of scented candles. In one end they could see a wooden counter and a sign above it that read, "Ye Olde Pizza Shoppe." A man with a puffy white hat was tossing dough in the air. The rest of the place seemed to be filled with gift items, although they did see one shelf of textbooks.

Ti approached the bored-looking teenager behind the cash register in the middle of the store, dressed in a colonial-era vest and tri-cornered hat, who was rearranging a display of quill pens on the counter. Ti flashed his best smile and said, "Excuse me, sir, but we need to break this hundred-dollar bill."

The boy didn't say anything. He just pointed to a sign, written in fancy calligraphy on parchment paper and framed on the wooden post behind him. It read, "No Change Giveneth Without a Purchase."

"What does that mean?" Brieahnaugh asked.

"It means you gots to buy somepin, Sista," Eagle said, "and bust up that Benjamin, so we can gets our coin."

"No way," said the freckled girl. "You're the ones who don't take credit cards. *You* need to buy something."

"Fine," Ti said, pointed his finger around the store. To his brothers he said, "We need to find the cheapest thing in here."

While the three girls went to the café in the back and used a credit card to order espressos and volcano water, the Faber brothers spread out through the store, looking for something cheap.

"What about thith?" Dixon yelled out a few minutes later. "I wanna buy thith!"

"What is it?" Ti asked, looking at the thick leather book Dixon was holding up.

"Ith a firsth edition of *The Birds of America*, by John James Audubon!"

"Dixon," Ti said, looking at the price-tag. "It's a hundred thousand dollars."

"Tho?"

"No."

They looked around for another twenty minutes, checking the prices on handmade crystal snow globes of Brimmingham Academy that cost $800, oil-and-canvas paintings of Benedict Brimmingham, the school's founder, for $1600, and martini glasses with the school seal etched in them, $139 for a set of four.

Finally Ti decided to ask. "Excuse me," he said to the boy behind the counter, who was now polishing a set of replica dueling pistols which, according to the sign on the display case, were exactly like the ones Benedict Brimmingham had used to shoot the owner of the land upon which he had built this school.

"Yeah?"

"Could you please tell me, what's the cheapest thing in here?"

"Golf ball." The boy pointed a limp finger at a case by the door and went back to his polishing.

Dixon found it. It was set in a blue case and embossed with the Brimmingham seal. It cost $13.25 with tax. They paid, took the change, and gave four twenty-dollar bills to the girls, who were now enjoying plates of Tiramisu-flavored foam.

This left the brothers with $62.80, just barely enough to pay Castelli on Wednesday.

Chapter 16

On Wednesday the three brothers skipped school again, not that anyone noticed. Their classes were so huge the teachers didn't bother to take attendance, and all the office staff had been cut. They needed to bring the money to Castelli, so they snuck into the nursing home and went looking for Johnny Fitziguzzi. They were hoping to borrow his electric wheelchair and shorten the 12-mile walk to the charter school.

Eventually they recognized a familiar sound—an old man singing Elvis songs loud and off-key—and found Johnny in a storage room behind the kitchen. Dressed in a beige jumpsuit and white patent-leather shoes, he was prying the lid off of a gallon-size can and pouring the contents into a paper shopping bag.

He didn't hear them come up behind him, so when Dixon asked him, "What are you doing, Mithter Fitziguzzi?" Johnny jumped.

He turned to face them, trying to hide the can behind his back. "What? What are you talking about? Nothing! Scram!"

"Tha's so Jam!" said Eagle. "You workin' a angle, ain'tchu, Mista Fits?"

"Yeah, yeah, but this is my deal," Johnny said. "Don't think you're gonna get a piece."

"Ith that coffee?" Dixon asked, looking in the paper bag and sniffing carefully. "It thmells like coffee. I'd thay a very low-grade blend, Chinethe probably, with non-coffee additives. I can thmell thawdust and roasted talcum powder."

"Yeah, it's coffee. I sell it to the guy at Bob's Kwikky Stop. I get two bucks a pound and a Slim Jim. You rat me out and I'll come into that bus one night while you're sleepin' and gut ya like a trout."

"Mmmm," Dixon. "Trout!"

Johnny lifted a bucket onto the counter.

"What's in there?" Ti asked.

"Bark mulch," Johnny said, and flashed a grin. His teeth were the color of aged banana skins. "It's fresh, right outa the garden."

He carefully poured its contents into the coffee can. Then he dusted the top with actual coffee from his shopping bag, replaced the lid, and put it back up on the shelf.

While he was taking down another can and opening it up Johnny said, "I'm doing this for their own good, y'know. Old people shouldn't be drinkin' coffee. Rots the knee joints. Besides, they can't taste the difference."

"That so *kareemy,* Yo!" Eagle said.

"What the hell is he saying?"

"Say, Mister Fitziguzzi. . ." Ti looked up at the old man with his most big-eyed, angelic smile.

"What is it now?"

"Do you think we could borrow your electric wheelchair? We need to go out to the charter school today to uh, do some business." Ti didn't want to tell him that they were paying Castelli; he knew Johnny would accuse them of being "soft."

Johnny Fitziguzzi didn't actually need an electric wheelchair—he could walk just fine—but he'd won it in a poker game, and he liked the attention he got when he rode it around downtown. He faced Ti and growled, "No!"

"How come?" Dixon asked. He looked hurt.

"How come? None a your stinkin' business. It just so happens I got a hot date today with a widow. She's eighty-nine, she's got a bad ticker, and I hear she's loaded. I'm gonna get my chair waxed and polished nice. Then I'm gonna take her for a little spin before we hit the early-bird special at Denny's. When she finds out I got wheels I'm gonna be in like Flynn."

It took the brothers nearly four hours to walk to the Hovering Parents Cooperative Community Charter School. They stopped for a while to eat peaches from a tree in front of a church until the priest came out, told them they'd burn in hell, and chased them away. In the woods by a stream Dixon filled the metal pot he always carried in his backpack with water, started a small fire of sticks, and made them all pine-needle tea. Then they really scored: behind a Pizza Hut they saw a pimply faced kid in a uniform toss a pizza box into the dumpster. When he'd gone back inside they opened the lid of the dumpster and pulled out the box. It was cold, but it was whole, covered with pineapple, broccoli, and anchovies.

Someone must have ordered it and never picked it up, and the ingredients had been too weird to resell.

Despite all that good food, when they arrived at the charter school Eagle collapsed onto one of the hand-hewn benches, exhausted.

"You're in terrible aerobic conditioning," Ti said to him.

"Is the bling, Brah. It weighs me down."

"So get rid of it."

"No way! How else I'ma look swagalicious for the ladies?"

It was so late in the day that school had ended. Now the students were having Enrichment, an after-school program. Under the shade of a massive maple tree, some kids banged drums in a circle while a bearded teacher strolled among them, strumming a lute.

On the lawn—this school, unlike Burr Oak Elementary, had grass—another group of kids had been playing non-competitive team hacky-sack. One of the fourth-graders, however, a boy with short, curly red hair and matching red suspenders, had accused one of the second-grade girls of what he called "pre-aggressive behavior," so the DOPEs had been called in. Now everyone was sitting in a circle, talking about how the pre-aggressive behavior made them feel.

"It almost hurt my feelings," the red-haired boy said, pouting.

"Yeah," said a boy next to him. "And when his feelings are almost hurt, that almost hurts *my* feelings."

"Very good, children," one of the DOPEs was saying, scribbing notes on a steno pad. "Does anybody else have feelings they'd like to share?"

"Shayam," Eagle said, watching this from the safety of some bushes. "How 'come in our school when someone's aggressive, the teachers hit them with rubber spatulas?"

"Because if they use rulers it leaves those red marks."

Dixon spotted Castelli in a remote corner behind the compost. She had a 5th grade boy with a long, blonde ponytail face down in the dirt. "If you so much as flinch I'll break all the bones in your toes," she was saying to him, "and you'll never play Ultimate Frisbee again." The boy's shirt was up around his shoulders. She was using colored Sharpies to draw a detailed picture of their charter school, right down to the rain-barrels, with a giant mushroom cloud exploding above it.

The brothers crouched behind a bin of rotting leaves and watched Castelli draw, afraid that if they disturbed her they'd get hurt. Today she had her hair in pigtails. She was wearing a black Porsche T-shirt and camouflage army fatigues. Ti thought he could see the outline of a pistol in one of her pockets.

Dixon gazed at her dreamily, pointed to her T-shirt, and said, "Ooooh. Nice car."

Ti said, "Dixon, shut up."

"Thorry." Dixon turned his back towards his brothers, pulled a black pen from his pocket and began quietly drawing on his arm.

"And . . . done," Castelli said several minutes later. She signed her name over the boy's hip bone with a big flourish. She stood up and the boy ran away, rearranging his shirt and brushing dirt off of his face. As he ran she yelled after him, "That's art, you know! If you ever wash it I'll break your nose, and you'll be so ugly you'll never get into another *a capella* group again!"

The Faber brothers continued to hide. Castelli shoved her pens back into a leather pouch, zipped the pouch into one of the pockets on her camo pants, and strode directly towards them.

"So," she said, crossing her arms and standing over them. "You brought me my money?"

They slowly looked up at her. None of them said anything. Eagle's hands were shaking.

"C'mon," Castelli barked. "Fork it over. I don't have all day. There's plenty more hippy kids I need to decorate before their parents get here."

Ti stood and pulled the plastic bag from his back pocket. "Here you go, Ma'am," he said meekly. "It's all there."

Castelli grabbed Eagle by the hoody and threw him to the ground. Then she jammed her elbow into the small of his back, causing him to go limp.

"Are you going to draw on him?" Dixon asked.

"No," Castelli said. "I'm gonna count on him." She tore open the bag and spread the crumpled bills and change around on Eagle's back. When she was done she carefully smoothed the bills, counted them, stacked them up, folded them, and shoved them into her back pocket. She brushed the quarters, dimes, nickels and pennies in the dirt and scowled, "I don't accept metal."

She stood up and pointed at the other two brothers. "Kneel!"

Ti and Dixon did.

Castelli reached behind her neck and grabbed the nunchuks from inside the back of her leather jacket. She pulled them apart hard, so that the metal chain snapped in front of their faces. Then she held one stick and spun the other so it whirred like helicopter blades inches from their heads.

"You trying to cheat me?!" Castelli yelled. The nunchuks continued to whir—over their heads, beside their ears, brushing their clothes.

"No Ma'am," Ti said, big-eyed and imploring. "It's all there, just like you said. Sixty-two fifty."

"You're a day late, punk," Castelli snarled. "It doubled. You owe me one-twenty-five."

"But you said we had a week, and that was Wednesday, and it's Wednesday today, so that's one week."

"A week is seven days, idiot. So it was due yesterday. You want me to draw a calendar on your face?"

"No thank you."

"Okay. So get me the money by Tuesday. That's *Tuesday*, got it? Otherwise it doubles again, and if you're late maybe this time I use my tattoo needles."

Dixon smiled at her lovingly and held out the arm he'd been drawing on. "I'd like a tattoo of *thith!*"

Castelli's nunchuks stopped spinning. She put them together and re-holstered them behind her neck. Then she grabbed Dixon's arm, pulled it towards herself, and peered at it.

"Who did this?" she demanded.

"Uh, uh . . ." Dixon was so afraid he couldn't speak.

"Was it *you?*"

Dixon just stammered.

"Did you do this? Come on! Speak up, you big oaf!"

"Y-y-y-yeth," Dixon said, almost crying. "It wath me."

"And this is a portrait of me, isn't it?"

"W-w-w-w—"

"Tell the truth or I'll smack you!"

"Yeth. It'th of you."

For the first time in six years, four months, and thirteen days, Castelli smiled. She put her arm around Dixon's shoulder, gazed at the drawing on his arm, and said, "Thank you. It's beautiful."

She dropped Dixon's arm and put a black-gloved finger in Ti's face. "But you still owe me a hundred and twenty five by Tuesday, short-stuff."

"We just gave you over sixty," Ti said.

"What sixty?" Castelli said. "I didn't see any sixty." She pointed her thumb over her shoulder at the nunchuks. "And if you've got a complaint about the service, you can take it up with Maim and Kill."

Chapter 17

It was now dark, cold, and past nine p.m., and the Faber brothers still hadn't made it home. They had run into Bernie the Zookeeper, who had been out of a job ever since the city had closed the zoo for lack of funds. They'd found him by the dump, where he'd gone to feed the raccoons.

"Why do you feed the raccoonth?" Dixon asked him as they walked. "They're like rats. But leth tasty."

"I love all the animals, Dixon," Bernie said. "Even the disgusting ones."

In front of the Kwikky Stop, the brothers said hello to Firechief Tony, who was sitting on a plastic bucket, taking swigs from a bottle of cookie-dough flavored schnapps.

"How ya doin'?!" Said Firechief Tony. He handed the bottle towards them. "You wanna hit?" Firechief Tony had in fact been the fire chief once, until the mayor of East Westford had tried to balance the budget by privatizing the fire department. Now fires were supposed to be put out by a private company called Blaz-B-Gon, which was located three towns away and staffed by untrained teenagers. Since then every house and building in East Westford that had caught fire ended up a blackened pile of rubble, and the trees were full of cats. It all made Firechief Tony so sad he'd taken to drink. And he still had his pension, so he was one of the lucky few who could afford to.

"I'll take one," Eagle said, reaching for the bottle, but Ti slapped it away.

"No you won't. We've got work to do."

"Man, Brah," Eagle said. "How 'come it's always work with you? Don't a homey ever get to *chill*?"

"Because we've got to raise a lot of money in a hurry," Ti said, "so we can finally pay back Castelli."

"Cathtelli likes me," Dixon said, gazing lovingly at the stars.

"Yes she does, Dixon," Ti said. "But she also seems to be mentally unbalanced."

"Yo, Brah," Eagle said to Ti. "You needs to relax yourself. All we gots to do is gank another load of them truffles from Wally World and sell them to them dope birds at Brimmingham."

"Okay," Ti said. "Let's go take orders."

"Now?"

"Now," Ti said.

"C'mon, Mang!" Eagle whined. "It's night time. Me wants to go watch *Jeopardy* through the windows at the Nursing Home."

"A wasted day is a day you can never get back," Ti said. "And so far, this is a wasted day." He and Dixon began to walk away towards the tunnel. "Come on."

"You go, Brah. I'ma stay here with Tony so's I can marinate."

"We can't do it without you, Eagle. We're a family."

"A crime family!" Dixon said.

Eagle crossed his arms and shook his head, no.

Ti gave him a look. "What do you think Angry Jonas," the worst bully on the bus, "would do to you if he found out you still sleep with a stuffed puppy?"

"You'd tell him about Fluffy Precious Foofoo?"

"I would."

"I'm comin'."

Once they'd crawled through the tunnel, the Faber brothers snuck across the Brimmingham campus, hiding behind bushes, statues, and the sides of buildings to escape the security forces, who patrolled at night with attack dogs and miniature robotic airplanes. Figuring it was around massage time, they made their way to the back of the William Howard Taft Center for Recreational Enrichment at Brimmingham Academy and used the platinum pass card Parker had given them to open a basement door.

Another swipe of the card opened the doors of the elevator, which whooshed them up to the eighth floor. Brieahnaugh and her friends, however, were not in the spa. Nobody was. They heard voices and followed them to the door of a closet. They knocked, and a woman with short blonde hair opened it a crack. Ti recognized her from the first time they'd come here; she was one of the massage ladies. In the room behind her he could see brooms, mops, buckets, shelves of towels, two other women in white uniforms, and three cots where they apparently slept.

"Massage Therapy ends at 9:30," a blonde woman said, and pointed to a neat little sign on the outside of the door. "We re-open in the morning at 6."

"Oh, we're not here for a massage," Ti said. "We're looking for that tall girl, Brieahnaugh, and her friends. They get a massage. Do you know them?"

The dark-skinned woman behind her snorted. "Oh yes, we know those three all right. They're here every night."

Ti noticed a slight edge in her voice. "They owe us money," Ti lied. "We need to collect."

"They owe us money too," the dark-skinned woman said, smiling. "About three years worth of tips!"

The third woman, who looked Hawaiian, laughed and they high-fived. "Like we'll ever see a dime of that!"

"Do you have any idea where they might be?" Ti asked.

"We sure do, sweetheart," said the blonde woman. "They're in the hospital."

"Karma!" said the dark-skinned woman, and laughed again.

"In Eatht Wethtford Memorial?" Dixon said, his eyebrows furrowed with worry. "Are they thtill alive?"

"Ha!" said the Hawaiian-looking woman. "You don't go to this school, do you?"

"Why do you ask?" Ti said.

"No matter. If you did you'd know that Brimmingham Academy has its *own* hospital. They're in the Richard Z. and Elizabeth A. Cheney Center for Medical Freedom, right past the first golf course, on your left. Look for the Plastic Surgery Wing."

It took the brothers a while to find it—they kept getting lost in the wrong golf course—but when they finally got to the enormous glass doors of the Richard Z. and Elizabeth A. Cheney Center for Medical Freedom they looked in and saw guards in black uniforms wearing bullet-proof vests, pistols in holsters, pacing back and forth in front of the entrance carrying shotguns.

"How are we supposed to get past *that*?" Ti wondered aloud.

"When they backs be turned we'll jump out of a bush and knock them out and hide them in a trash can," Eagle said.

"Because that worked so well with Castelli?" Ti said. "And she only had a couple of wooden sticks?"

"Mmmmm," Dixon said dreamily. "She'th an artist, like me."

"Why you always dissin' my ideas, Dawg?" Eagle said to Ti.

"I don't know, Eagle," Ti said sweetly. "But one possibility might be that they suck."

"You got a better one?"

"Actually, yes I do. I was thinking we go around back, where there's probably a servant's entrance or something, and use the platinum card."

"Jam!" Eagle said. "Why didn't I think of that?"

"Because you're thilly?" Dixon suggested.

Eagle said, "I wasn't really looking for an answer."

They did in fact find a back entrance with a loading dock and a door for employees. Three workers were unloading a truck filled with cases marked "Vozz Artesian Water. It's from Norway, so you know it's good for you."

As the brothers walked past them into the building, one of the workers said to another, "Can you believe they bathe in this stuff?"

"That was easy," Ti said a bit smugly as they stood in a small windowless room at the end of a hallway. There was nothing else in the room except a thick metal elevator door and an electronic keypad on the wall next to it.

Eagle swiped the platinum card along the reader at the side of the keypad, and letters scrolled across the screen.

"Shayam!" Eagle scowled. He read the words aloud: "No permission found."

"Try it again," Ti suggested.

Same result.

"You kids are supposed to be here, right?" called one of the workers in the loading dock.

"Oh yeah, Yo," Eagle said.

"We're visiting some sick friends," Ti explained.

"At one in the morning?" the man asked.

"We just got out of golf class."

"Ah," said the man. He shook his head and went back to work.

"Hurry up," Dixon said. "That guy's on to uth!"

"Hurry up?" Eagle said. "Hurry up and do what? The card don't work, Brah! I told you this idea was crunk."

"No you didn't," Dixon said.

"Well, I meant to. But I did tell you we should take out them guards at the front door and stuff 'em in trash cans, and you said 'No, that's a dumb idea,' and you shamed me, Brah. You shamed your own homeboy. You made me feel *small*."

"I'm sorry," Ti said, not really meaning it.

"You should be, Brah," Eagle said, getting louder and louder. "You should be. Because I had a creamy plan, a dope plan, it maybe still had a few kinks to work out, but it was solid. And you didn't work with me to make it better. You didn't even offer up any suggestions, like using poison knock-out gas, or dressing up as Ninjas and swooping down from the ceiling, or somepin like that. No, no, you just shut me down. And now here we are in this scary little box of a room with a crazy loading-dock guy ready to put us in the slamma and no way past this door because our card can't get us through this Intel 531 Blue Magnum Security Interface. Whataya think about that? Huh, Mang?"

Ti waited until he was done. Then he paused, smiled, and said very calmly and quietly, "Do you really want to know what I think? I think you should do that special computer voodoo that you do so well."

"Oh yeah . . ."

Eagle pulled an old iPod out of a pocket in his hoody, then found some wires in another pocket. He plugged something into the phone's port, clipped something else to something on the side of the electronic keypad, and punched buttons on his phone.

"Here it is," he said, sounding sinister. "The visitor's list. We'll just add ourselves to that and jet. What name should we use, Brahs? Swaggy McShizzle? M.C. Blingbling?"

"Shouldn't we use Parker Worthington? Since that's the name on the card?"

"Oh yeah," Eagle said. He punched some more buttons on the phone, then hit 'Enter' with a flourish. "There! Now we be all lunky dunky!"

Sure enough, the next time he swiped the card the elevator doors pinged and opened up. They strolled in.

"Have a nice visit!" said the man from the loading dock.

Once they were in the elevator, however, the doors closed automatically behind them, locked with a click, and didn't move.

They looked around. There were no buttons, levers, instructions, anything—except posters advertising a sale on Botox injections and the new menu at the hospital restaurant, which had recently earned its second Michelin star.

They were trapped.

Chapter 18

"Yo, homeys," Eagle said. "This be buggin'! We headed for the slammer fo' sho."

Dixon said, "What do we do?"

"I don't know," Ti said.

They searched all four walls of the elevator, sweeping the surfaces with their hands. Nothing.

Eagle began to panic. "These richies gonna use us to do experiments on," he whined. "I heard about it from M.C. Larry. They takes homeys out the jails, they shoot 'em up with experimental drugs, and they turn 'em into chimpanzees!"

"That'th thilly," Dixon said. "Don't be thilly, Eagle."

"Yeah," Ti said nervously. "Try to *help*."

They heard a chime like a doorbell. Then a female, robotic voice from above said cheerfully, "Welcome to the Help Menu."

"Oh, hi," Ti said.

"Wassup," Eagle said.

"How. May I. Help You."

"Uh, Plastic surgery please," Ti said in a small voice.

"Plastic. Surgery. Searching…" They heard a whirring noise. Then after a while the female robot voice said, "Three. Results found for. Plastic. Surgery? Please. Specify."

"Specify?" Ti said aloud to his brothers. "I don't know which one. Do you guys?"

"The expensivest one?" Dixon guessed.

"Yeah, that's the shizzle," Eagle said.

"Most expensive plastic surgery!" Ti yelled at the ceiling. "Deluxe. Premium. Fancy."

Suddenly the floor jolted and they began moving upward. "Thank you. For choosing. Brimmingham Academy. Your tax-free donations are. Important to us. Have. A nice. Day."

The 14th floor was beautiful: oak floors, oriental rugs, crystal chandeliers, the ceilings painted with angels and clouds.

Dixon saw something on the mahogany wall and stomped over to it. He examined it closely for a while, then turned to a nurse who was sitting behind a marble desk.

"Ith thith a real Picatho?" he asked. "From his Rose period?"

The nurse was probably in her seventies, but she had bright yellow hair and skin pulled so tight over her face that it made her mouth look like a wide, horizontal line. "Yes, it is a Picasso," she said. "1904. It's considered to be his first use of the harlequin."

"Yo, sista!" Eagle said to her. "Where our brizzie brizzle Brieahnaugh be at?"

The nurse gazed intently at Eagle for a while. Then she said, "Do you boys have an appointment?"

Ti turned on his power smile and sidled up to the front of her desk.

"Hi," he said charmingly.

"Hello," the nurse said back.

"I'm Parker Worthington," he said, and passed the platinum ID card over the polished marble towards her.

She ran it through the side of her computer, and peered at the screen for a while. She looked like she was having trouble focusing.

"You're 16?"

"*Sweet* sixteen, I like to think," Ti said.

"You don't look 16."

"It's an old photo."

"Ah."

"And I'm old enough to know that I'd like to do shots with *you* when you turn twenty-one."

"What kind of shots? Botox?"

"I was thinking more like gin."

The nurse put her hand over her mouth and giggled. "Oh, you. You're a charmer, aren't you?"

"Hey," said Ti, batting his long eyelashes, "I can tell a good-looking college student when I see one."

The nurse smiled as best she could without tearing the skin on her face and pressed a button under the surface of her desk. A panel of the wall at one end of the corridor swung open to reveal a door.

"They're in Room 14368."

As his brothers followed Ti towards the door, however, the nurse said, "Wait a second!"

They all turned to look at her.

"Who are these two?"

This made Dixon and Eagle nervous.

"Altho Parker Worthington?" Dixon asked, looking at his feet.

The nurse's eyebrows scrunched together. "All three of you?"

"In a manner of speaking," Ti said with a fake laugh. "They're my personal assistants. They have been since I was born. So as far as they're concerned, they really don't have names of their own."

"Oh," said the nurse. "Of course."

The brothers walked down the carpet-covered corridors for what seemed like ten minutes, admiring the paintings, shotguns, and framed "first-ever Botox needle" on the walls. Finally they found Brieahnaugh's room. Her name had been painted on the mahogany door in gold paint, along with the names of her two friends.

They entered a room that reminded them of pictures they'd seen of the Oval Office. It was huge, with paneled walls, carpets, fancy furniture, and at the far end of a dining room, kitchen, and lounge area, crackling logs in the fireplace. Each of the three girls lay in her own big, fluffy bed, faces bandaged. They were sipping smoothies through silver straws from tall glasses while a *Twilight* movie played on the giant flat-screen TV across from them. The girls weren't watching it, however; they were each staring intently at their phones and texting with their thumbs.

Ti noticed that each girl's feet protruded from under the covers and rested in special wooden devices, padded and covered with green velvet, that held their ankles stable and spread their toes. Attendants in white uniforms sat on stools at the ends of their beds, painting their toenails.

Dixon rushed over to the full bar and kitchen in the far corner and opened the fridge. He called over to the girls, "Hey, do you know, are these croithants all-butter? The ones made with partially-hydrogenated cotton-theed oil give me hives."

The freckled girl looked up from her texting and noticed them for the first time. She screamed, "You *monsters!*"

A door at the far end of the room opened up to reveal men in black body armor and helmets, pointing stun guns.

"Permission to taze?" asked on of the guards.

"Denied," Brieahnaugh said, bored, looking up from her phone. "Go *away*."

"Sorry to disturb you, Ma'am," the guard said.

"You better be," Brieahnaugh said. "That's like the fifth time today."

The guards retreated back behind the door and closed it carefully.

"Why didn't you have them tazed?" the freckled girl said to Brieahnaugh. "They like, ruined our faces. They should be tortured."

"Because," Brieahnaugh said. "It'll be more fun to torture them ourselves."

"I knew we was gonna get experimented on," Eagle said. "These brizzies gonna turn us into chimps!"

"Worse!" Brieahnaugh said. "We're going to turn you into social outcasts."

"Excuthe me!" Dixon called over from the kitchen area. "Do you want eggs? I wath thinking I'd dip the croithants in egg batter to make a kind of a new-thtyle *croque monsieur*."

"Wha's that, Brah?" Eagle called over to him.

Dixon explained. "Croque monsieur ith like French toatht with ham and melted cheese. It'th extraordinary. I plan to use thith very nice thmoked thalmon with Camenbert."

"I'm in," Eagle said.

"Me, too," said Ti.

"Girlth?" asked Dixon.

"Shut up!" Brieahnaugh yelled. "We're trying to torture you."

"Why that, sista?" Eagle asked. "We never done you no non-good."

"Huh?"

"We been straight up! We bring you the shizzle! Thas why we here. We wanna know if you wanna buy some more of them snorky white-chocolate truffles. For your faces and all."

"Well for your information," said the emaciated girl, "Your so-called *shizzle* gave us blemishes. Why do you think we're even *in* this hospital?"

"I thought it wath to fatten you up," Dixon said from the kitchen. "You look tho hungry."

"No," she said. "Your product ruined our skin."

"Well whataya want, Sista? You was rubbin' chocolate on your face!"

"That's not what gave us blemishes," Brieahnaugh said huffily. "It was the ants." She lifted the bandage on her forehead to reveal beautiful, cappuccino-colored skin, and one tiny red spot.

"Ants?"

"Yes," the freckled girl said indignantly. "While we were moon tanning with your product on our faces, we were attacked by bees and ants."

"Could you please explain?" Ti said politely. "What's moon tanning?"

"Getting a tan from the moon," Brieahnaugh said. "At night. Stupid."

"Well then I guess you shouldn't a been wearin' that tweak. Maybe you should be *eatin'* it, like everybody else."

"You don't understand our issues," the freckled girl said.

"How can he?" said the starved-looking one. "He's *poor.*"

"If your product wasn't made to be worn while moon tanning," said Brieahnaugh, "why wasn't that warning clearly stated on the label?"

"Yeah!" said the freckled one.

"You probably got the wrong kind of white chocolate," said the frighteningly skinny one. "It probably wasn't Swiss. I bet it was counterfeit Swiss. It was probably from *England* or something."

"I had thix of them," Dixon said cheerily from the kitchen, "And they were definitely Thwiss."

"Which is why," said Brieahnaugh, ignoring him, "we are going to torture you. We're going to tell everybody who's important that you're *not* important, and we're going to tell them that you're *tacky.* That means you won't get invited to any good parties, and you won't have any service on your phone. You'll wish you were dead."

"Plus," said the bony one, "our dads are going to *sue* you."

"Sue us for what?" Eagle asked, amazed. "We don't own nothin' you can take. We don't even got a crib."

"You don't?" Brieahnaugh asked, confused. "Then we'll take your cars."

"Don't have one," Ti said.

"Boats?" suggested the freckled one.

"Once I carved a boat out of a winter-melon I found behind the thupermarket!" Dixon said. "I used it to make winter-melon thoup!"

"Then we'll take all your jewelry," the frighteningly thin girl said. "And sell it!"

"I already tried that," Eagle said, "but Frankie at the pawn shop says there ain't no market for plastic. Can you believe that crunk?"

While Dixon was delivering the sandwiches to his brothers on gold-decorated ceramic plates, the girls began furiously texting with their thumbs.

After a while the freckled girl read a text, looked over at Brieahnaugh, and said to her, "L. O. L."

"What?" said Dixon, biting into his second croissant sandwich.

"We've decided," Brieahnaugh said, smiling maliciously, "that we're going to sell you three idiots to the hospital, so they can do experiments on you."

Chapter 19

"Guards!" Brieahnaugh shrieked. "Taze them!"

The door at the far end of the room banged open again, and out jumped the two armed guards, raising their Tazer rifles to their eyes.

Ti yelled, "Run!"

Dixon shoved the last croissant sandwich into his mouth and lumbered after his two brothers towards the door.

Dixon couldn't run very fast, but neither could the guards in their heavy armor, and the guards had much farther to run from their closets at the far end of the room through the dining and lounge areas.

The freckled girl could see that the brothers were about to get away: They were already opening the door, while the guards were still stumbling around an antique sofa. "They're escaping!" she shrieked. "Stop them!"

Her skeleton-like friend was too hungry to move, but Brieahnaugh tried to slide out of bed. Her toes were still locked into the nail-polishing devices, however, so she fell with a thump to the thick carpet.

The freckled girl realized it was all up to her. Using the technique that had made her captain of Brimmingham Academy's figure-skating team, she leaped from her bed, performed a perfect double-Axel (degree of difficulty 1.0), and landed on Dixon's back.

At the same time she was sinking her newly painted talons into Dixon's shoulder-blades, however, the guards tripped over a Chippendale tea table and accidentally fired their weapons. One Taser dart landed in the left cheek of a toe-nail technician. The other landed in the butt of the freckled girl.

Both women screamed and fell to the ground, where they lay twitching.

By now the brothers were running down the hallway. It was extremely long, with rows of doors and paintings and thick carpet and no ends or exits in sight. High on the walls, red lights were flashing. They could hear a gentle female voice coming from dozens of unseen speakers saying, "Condition Ruby, please! Ruby! Freedom Brigade to Floor Fourteen for Condition Ruby!"

Finally the brothers came to an intersection. Should they go left? Right? Or straight ahead? Each direction looked the same: just a long, well-carpeted hallway.

"Go left," Dixon said.

His brothers did, and saw twelve guards in black uniforms running towards them. The guards had the letters "F B" on the fronts of their black combat helmets and armor. One of them pointed a bright yellow Taser rifle at Eagle, who was in front. Eagle watched a green laser dot move up his chest to his forehead, then back down his chest to his boy parts.

"It's the jakes!" Eagle yelled. "An' they shootin' for my wang-dang! Go the other way!"

The brothers turned and sprinted back to the intersection. They could see more Freedom Brigade guards to their left, and to the right, the two guards now lumbering up from Brieahnaugh's room. The only clear hallway was straight ahead, so they ran down it. And down it. And down it. This seemed like a good thing, that it was so long, because it allowed them to create more distance between themselves and the slower-moving guards. Then they heard a police radio squawk somewhere, and a male voice said, "We've got them cornered, sir. They're headed down the Jane Rivers Memorial Deep Plane Face-Lift Wing, and there's no getting out of that one."

"Shayam!" Eagle yelled when they reached the dead end. He stomped his foot and flashed a few of his would-be gang signs. "I guess the pork chops got us now. We gonna be experimented on."

"No they don't," Dixon said, opening what looked like an oven door in one of the walls.

"That says 'debris,' Dixon," Ti said, pointing to a small sign on the wall above it. "That's a fancy word for garbage."

"I know," Dixon said. "And it thmells exquisite!"

He was the largest of them by far, but Dixon pulled the door fully open and jumped in, hands in front of him like an Olympic diver. He just barely squeezed through.

"That's disgusting," Ti said, scrunching up his nose. "It'll get my suit dirty."

Eagle looked at him: Ti's "suit" t-shirt was already covered with croissant crumbs. "Hey Brah," Eagle said, and pointed up the hallway at the black-clad guards pounding towards them. "Smell the bacon. It's this or a cage in the laboratory, drinkin' water out of hamster bottle."

Eagle grabbed Ti by the back of his pants, pulled open the door, and shoved him in.

He could hear screaming.

"Sayonara, Porkers!" Eagle yelled. Then he jumped, too.

When Brieahnaugh finally arrived at the end of the Jane Rivers Memorial Deep Plane Face-Lift Wing she was out of breath, dressed in a white silk bathrobe with the school crest monogrammed on a breast pocket and the cotton balls from her toe-nail painting still between her toes. She found a crowd of guards in black riot gear staring at a small door in the wall labeled "debris."

"Well?" she said, hands on her hips. "Where are they?"

"They've gone down that trash hole, Ma'am," the head of the guards said.

"Then go in after them and get them!" she barked.

"But it's dirty in there, Ma'am," the guard said.

"So?"

"No need," another guard explained. "This chute goes straight down to the furnace in the basement. It's two thousand degrees Fahrenheit. By now all the BTUs in those boys' bodies have been converted to heat and used to warm up the outdoor mud baths. There's nothing left of them but ashes and dust."

"Dang it!" Brieahnaugh said, and stamped her newly painted toes on the carpet. "I wanted to torture them some more."

Chapter 20

The chute, however, no longer went to the incinerator. Three years earlier, after another pay cut, some of the workers got to talking about the high quality of what was tossed into the garbage at the Richard Z. and Elizabeth A. Cheney Center for Medical Freedom. Sometimes food went down the chute still as it had been prepared in the kitchens, on fine china, covered with metal domes and aluminum foil embossed with the school seal. Sometimes the more senile of the Brimmingham patients, who got an alumni discount on joint replacements and liposuction, thought that the garbage doors were mail slots or safes, and threw down birthday cards filled with money intended for their grandchildren or a Patek-Phillipe watch.

So a few enterprising janitors had diverted the chute to a wide table in the basement, where they and their friends sorted the coffee cups, old newspapers, and soda cans from the full dinners, golf clubs, and pearl necklaces.

When Eagle fell with a plop on a pile of soda cans and champagne bottles in the middle of this sorting table, he used his sleeve to wipe dirty tissues and slime from his face. Dixon was sitting in a corner of the table, surrounded by what must have been forty boxed lunches. The boxes were made of gilded metal and decorated with the Cheney Center's crest and motto: *E Pluribus Pecuniam*.

"Can you believe it?" Dixon said to him. "The thilly rich folkth don't know how to eat a lobthter! They take out the tailth, but they leave behind the thweetest meat of all, in the clawth!"

Dixon had already opened several of the boxes, and was now gleefully ripping the knuckles and claws off the lobsters, cracking open the shells in his hands, and shoving the succulent pink meat into his mouth.

Ti, meanwhile, had found a plate covered in plastic wrap containing six strawberry tarts, and had already eaten three of them. He was now walking around the edges of the table, pawing through the trash.

Eagle had found a bag of "Organic Valencia Blood Oranges Imported From Barcelona" and was peeling one when his younger brother yelled, "Score!"

Ti held up a piece of fancy paper with writing and printing and a golden seal in one corner.

"What's that?"

"It's a certificate for a thousand shares of stock." He examined it more closely. "Never mind. It's for some company I've never heard of, called Facebook. It's probably worthless." He nonetheless placed it on the pile of treasures he'd already accumulated: a cedar box of Cuban cigars, a pair of Ralph Lauren sunglasses, a shiny chrome pistol, and an unopened bottle of 32-year-old Lagavulin single-malt scotch.

When the brothers first arrived at Parker Worthington's window, they could hear him yelling inside. "Slam that shuttlecock!" he shrieked. "Yes! Yes! Drive it! Bang it home!"

Dixon said to Eagle, "Do you think thith ith a bad time?"

"Too bad!" Eagle said. "This is an emergency."

When Parker finally heard them rapping on the glass and opened the window, he seemed happy to see them. He said, "How kind of you to stop in, Eagle, my curiously odiferous friend, and to bring your fraternal comrades."

Inside, Parker explained that he had been in the middle of two things: He'd been simultaneously watching a private video feed of a badminton tournament and wagering on the matches via a betting site on his open laptop.

Parker sniffed at the garbage and filth on their faces and clothes and asked if they would like him to summon the attendants and have them bathed. All three brothers gladly agreed. When they'd emerged from their baths in Brimmingham bathrobes, their fingernails buffed and their hair newly trimmed, they'd found that the attendants had also washed, ironed, and repaired their clothes.

"I'd like to repay your generous hospitality," Ti said. He held up the briefcase he'd found in the hospital debris pile, which now contained his treasures. "Does any of this interest you? Help yourself to any of it, except the scotch. I'm saving that for my dad."

"And the fo'fo!" Eagle said, pointing to the handgun Ti had found. "I's needin' that to cap Jonas."

"Who might Jonas be?" Parker asked.

"He's in second grade," Ti said.

Eagle glared at him. "He may be a shorty, but he the meanest bully on our bus."

Parker Worthington examined the items in Ti's briefcase. "This silver pen is actually plated, and thus not up to my standards, but when you write with it I hope you think of me." He squinted, then read a name he saw engraved on its side: "Or rather of Lowell Athol Peabody the Third," who had apparently tossed it down the Brimmingham hospital garbage chute.

He picked up the sunglasses. "Ralph Lauren," Parker sniffed. "He emblazons all of his clothing with the symbol of the polo player, the greatest sports hero in Anglo-Saxon history. Yet he himself was born in Brooklyn, his money is new, and he probably doesn't know a polo chukka from a pile of up-chuck." He tossed the glasses back in Ti's case.

"These, however, are lovely," Parker said. He ran one of the Cuban cigars under his nose and sniffed. "Monterrey Double Coronas. They're legendary, and absolutely breathtaking, but illegal to purchase in this country. How ever did you manage to get them?"

"I found them in a garbage chute," Ti said.

"You are too funny!" Parker chuckled, and patted him good-naturedly on the back. "I understand. We all have our secret sources, and you don't want to reveal yours. Fair enough." He looked up at the enormous screen on one wall of the room. "Oh! The next match is beginning. I'll smoke one, if you don't mind, after I've won."

Ti and Eagle sat down in Parker's maroon-leather arm chairs to watch him watch badminton while Dixon went to work on a chocolate-raspberry soufflé.

Up on the giant screen, they could see four players playing on a luxurious wooden court. On one side of the screen, a young man and woman dressed in crimson shirts and shorts smacked a white blur over a five-foot high net at a young man and woman dressed in dark blue shirts and shorts.

"Harvard Yale!" Parker said enthusiastically. "A truly riveting match-up!" He pointed to the woman in red. "Do you see this fetching maiden, Donatella Dole? She set Harvard's record for most points scored on a rainy Tuesday. Her family and my family own neighboring islands in the Dutch Antilles. We're great friends."

He pointed to her partner. "Zhi Peng Li, who you see here, is ranked third in the world. His father was accused of selling uranium to the North Koreans, but I don't believe it. I've met him, and he's a lovely chap. Of course, my grandpapa says the same thing about Mussolini."

They sat and watched while Parker described the game's fine points. "Notice the delicate, tumbling, net return," he said. "And that powerful, jumping smash."

Parker clicked away at the Macbook 300000 in his lap. He said, "I'm going to wager ten thousand dollars that Harvard wins the next point."

Dixon, however, was at that exact moment carrying over a tray of crab meat in puff pastry. He accidentally tripped over the head of a bear-skin rug and bumped into Parker's arm.

"Drat," Parker said calmly.

"Wassup, Brah?" Eagle asked.

"Because of that unfortunate collision with your brother, I hit the wrong button and lost five thousand dollars."

Dixon looked broken-hearted. A tear began rolling down his cheek. "I'm tho, tho, thorry," he said. "I'll pay you back."

"No, no, don't be silly," Parker said. "Accidents happen. Here:" He clicked a few more keys on his laptop. "I've just bet ten thousand that they'll lose the next point, with three-to-one odds."

The four players on the big screen flicked their rackets, jumped, smashed, and returned the little white thing across the net repeatedly, until Donatella hit it too far.

"There now," Parker said. "I just made thirty thousand. And I didn't even tell her to do that!"

When the match was over and Parker was leaning back in his club chair, luxuriously smoking one of Ti's cigars, he had made a total of $22,483.13 on IvyWager.com, tax free.

"So how 'bout you give some a that kareemy cash to us, Brah," Eagle suggested. "We in some serious crunk."

"Excuse me?" Parker said.

"Well you got all that green comin' in, and all we gots is debts goin' out. Maybe you could loan us a grand."

"But Eagle, my friend," Parker said. "If I were to loan you money, then how would you ever learn the meaning of hard work?"

"I sees your point, Brah," Eagle said.

Ti carefully explained to Parker the predicament they were in: If they didn't pay Castelli $125 by Tuesday she was going to break their legs with her nunchuks.

"My goodness," Parker said thoughtfully, puffing on his cigar. "That's such a small sum. It wouldn't even buy a decent pair of socks. Why don't you borrow the money from your daddy?"

"He be sick," Eagle said. "And he ain't got no coin."

"Your mumsy?"

Eagle explained that she'd died.

"Aunties?"

"Got none."

"Your grandpapa?"

"He thinks he's a giraffe. He literally *eats* money."

"Then I suppose you'll have to borrow from a friend."

"You're our only friend who has more than four dollars."

"Yes, but that's because my ancestors earned it, through hard work."

"How 'bout this," Eagle said. "How 'bout we boost you something? Don't you need us to jack you a case of champagne, or a Bimmer, or a puppy?"

"That's actually a smashing idea, my hip-hop hooligan," Parker said. "I purchase my liquors through my wine merchant, I prefer ponies to puppies, and I purchase my autos online. But as it happens, I am struggling a bit to take delivery of some important contraband."

"What'th a contraband?" Dixon asked as he served the soufflé.

"In this case," Parker explained, "about eighty pounds of explosives. Which FedEx refuses to deliver. We are dreadfully over-regulated by the socialists in our government."

Parker explained that his suite-mate, Francisco Antonia, had just earned his first billion, thanks to a wise bet on opium futures. Parker wanted to throw him a little celebration. He'd already printed the invitations, ordered the "bubbly," and hired the caterers. "But there is one thing missing," he said, stroking another cigar with his tongue.

"Explothives!" Dixon said.

"That so kareemy, Brah! You gonna blow up some buildings at Brimmingham? Maybe the emperor's house?"

"*Fireworks*, my simple, excitable darlings," Parker said, clipping the end off the cigar and lighting it up. "I'd pay you handsomely if you can procure for me through your underworld connections everything on this list."

He showed them a file on his laptop.

Ti jotted things down in the little notebook he always carried. "Ten dozen Obliterators, 25 dozen Nuke-a-Bams, but only the kind that contains actual spent nuclear fuel, thirty pounds of ExplodoMortars, and 100 assorted Tinkerbell Rainbows. Got it."

Chapter 21

Sean took four pills from the No-Doze dispenser mounted to the wall of the Security Center, tossed them into his mouth, and washed them down with a swig from his bucket of coffee. His left foot was wiggling like a marionette. "Jeeze," he said to himself, scratching hard at the stubble behind his ear. "It's them freak kids again."

He zoomed in the cameras that covered Wally World's Explosives Department. This time the giant-sized kid was wearing a Superman tank-top he must have owned for seven years, because it was so small it stopped above his belly button, and the cloth was thin enough in places that you could see through it. Apparently the kid had tried to disguise himself, because he had a trash bag tied around his head so that he could barely see. The hip hop nitwit, meanwhile, wore a football helmet from about the 1950s, still covered with mud from the dump where he must have dug it up. And the midget was the weirdest looking of them all: On his head he was wearing a plastic Halloween pumpkin with cut-outs for the eyes. He had a bow tie clipped to the front of his t-shirt, and he was carrying a leather briefcase. 'Krikey,' Sean thought. 'If you're tryin' to disguise yourself, why would you dress up like it's Halloween?'

Sean watched them over the monitors as the gangsta twit pushed a shopping cart and the shrimp kept looking at a list and pulling stuff off the shelves. When they were done, boxes of fireworks filled their cart so full that the gangsta couldn't even see where he was going. He kept crashing into things, knocking over shotguns and dynamite in the end-of aisle displays. The big guy, meanwhile, had spent a lot of time in the produce department. He must have squeezed every banana in the rack by the time the midget yelled something at him and pointed towards the check out. The big guy picked one and followed along.

Sean zoomed in the cameras by the cash registers and turned on the microphones. Biggy was carefully peeling his banana. He ate the entire thing in two bites, but held onto the peel. When their cart was finally at the front of the line and the

Monetary Associate was zapping their purchases with her scanner, the big oaf tossed his peel on the floor, stepped on it, and did the worst prat-fall Sean had ever seen.

"Ow, ow, I tripped and falled!" He lay on the floor, whining like a big baby, clutching at his thigh. "My thkin ith broken! I've thnapped my pancreatic! Call a lawyer!"

During the commotion—some old lady offered to help, while the Monetary Associate called a manager on her microphone—the shrimp and Mr. Hip-hop high-tailed it out the automatic doors with their shopping cart. Once they were safely outside, sure enough, the jolly pink giant miraculously recovered and ran after them.

Then, right outside the front doors, the three delinquents did their usual: They pulled off their dumb disguises and started in with the chest bumps and the cheering. Sean could understand, kinda; they'd gotten away with this two times before, so by now they probably thought they were good at it. Well, not this time. Not on his watch. He took another drink from his coffee bucket, and this time he pushed the big red button in the middle of his security console.

Out on the sidewalk, Ti was just starting his celebration speech—"Gentlemen, I want to congratulate you on our third successful liberation operation—" when on all four sides of them gates popped up out of the pavement, caging them in. Red lights above the automatic doors flashed, and sirens wailed.

Dixon yelled, "Follow me! Over the top!" He ran at the gates. He had intended to climb up on them and pull his brothers over, but when he touched the black metal his hand sparked bluish-white light. He bounced backwards and screamed. It was electrified.

"Turn the cart over!" Ti told Eagle, and for once his brother complied. "Now take off your hoodie and throw it over the metal!"

"But this be designer!"

"Kmart designer," Ti said. "Do it!"

"Fine!" Eagle said, "Sheesh." He pulled it off, hopped up onto the top of the cart, and had just thrown the hoodie over the top of the gate when Sean, watching this on the monitor, pressed a smaller black button next to the big red one that was labeled, "Deluxe."

Sean wove his hands behind his head and leaned back in his chair, smiling at the scene that now played out on the screens before him. First the nets dropped. Then the pepper spray shot up out of the pavement at such velocity that it knocked all three of the little thieves into a pile in the middle of the cage. He could tell the spray was working by the way the brats grabbed at their eyes and rolled around in pain.

Next he launched the blue dye bombs, which exploded all around them and made them look like three writhing Smurfs. Then, just to be sure, he hit them with the knock-out gas.

Some of the gas got picked up on the breeze and inhaled by an old Greeter guy who was just coming in for the second shift. He collapsed onto the pavement and cut open his chin on the curbstone. 'Hey, whataya want,' Sean said to himself, as a puddle of blood grew beneath the old gent. He took another swallow of coffee and hit the blue "health" button to summon the nurse. 'You're gonna get civilian casualties in every war.'

When Ti woke up, he couldn't see out of the puffy fires that had once been his eyes. He felt like he'd been stung in the face by a thousand angry wasps, and his eyelids had become water balloons coated with hot sauce.

"Here," said a gruff voice in front of him. "Rub this on your eyes."

"What is it?" Ti asked. He could feel somebody put a square of something soft and gooey in his hand.

"Cream cheese," said the voice.

"What kinda cream cheethe?" he could hear Dixon ask.

"How the hell should I know?" said the gruff voice. "It's Wally World brand."

"It'th not Organic Valley? Or Horizon? 'Cause I don't like the kind that's full of carrageenan. That thtuff's disguthting."

"Look, Smartass," the voice said. "ya rub this product on your eyes, I don't know if it's got carrageenan in it or friggin' plutonium, it cuts down on the burning."

Ti did as the voice had suggested: he rubbed the block of goo over his eyes, and gradually some of the burning and swelling went down enough that he could see a little through narrow slits. He and his brothers seemed to be sitting on chairs in a cement basement. The room smelled like mold. He could hear a dripping faucet somewhere behind him, and loud machinery. He had noticed that he could not move his feet; when he looked down he could see that they'd been taped to the legs of the chair with silver duct tape. It was the same for his brothers.

In front of him Ti could see a wiry little man with a grey buzz-cut, dressed in a bright orange uniform. The man paced so rapidly back and forth across the concrete that his sneakers squeaked. He was drinking something from a mug the size of a waste basket.

"You want a rock star?" the man said.

"No," Ti said, misunderstanding him. "I'm hoping to become a hedge-fund manager. Or a crime boss."

"Huh?" said the man, confused. "No, not 'do you want to be a rock star.' Do you wanna drink a Rockstar?" He pointed a skinny black can at Ti.

"Don't do it!" Dixon yelled. "Ith loaded with thucrose!"

"I likes it!" Eagle said, talking very fast. Ti could see that he was holding a similar can in his duct-taped hands. "I likes it a lot. I think it has a kareemy taste wit a buzz like a big ole dose o' cold medicine!"

"Shut up, kid," said the buzz-cut man. "You can't handle it. You're cut off." He yanked the can away from Eagle, finished it himself, then tossed it in a corner, where it clattered against the cement.

"No, mang! I likes it! C'mon! Gimme another. Please please please? Just one more!"

Sean pulled a canister from his utility belt, pointed it into Eagle's face, and pressed the button with his index finger. A spray of white foam covered his nose and mouth.

"God, I hate gangstas," he said, "with their baggy pants and the gold in their mouth."

Eagle slobbered a few times and passed out. His brothers gasped.

"What are you going to do to us?" Ti asked nervously. "Please don't kill us."

"Ha!" the man laughed. "Kill ya. That's a good one. I just saved your heinies."

"You did?"

"Yeah. The Assistant to the Assistant Manager wanted to send you off to maximum-security juvenile jail. But I said no. I said I'd vouch for you kids."

"How come?"

"I knew your mother, that's why."

"You did?"

"Sure I did. We rode the same bus."

"Didn't everybody ride the same bus?"

"No no, small fry. Back then they had five or six busses for each school. Every kid got their own seat. It was good."

"Were you friends with her? Was she nice?" Their mother had died four years earlier, and Ti didn't remember her very well.

"She was wicked nice, little fella. Wicked nice. And beautiful, with long, dark, wavy hair and skin the color of latte. And that little accent of hers . . . Italian, right?"

"Sort-of," Ti said. "She was born in the Italian part of Switzerland. Locarno."

"She was real classy and elegant," the man said. "And she had a wicked right hook, too."

"You mean, like a punch?"

"A helluva punch. One time when Davey Johnson was pickin' on me, it was about the fifth time that week, he was always on me, stealin' my lunch, knockin' over my books, peein' on my coat, trippin' me when I got on the bus, trippin' me when I got off the bus, stickin' my head into trash cans, stickin' my head into toilets, givin' me wedgies—well anyhow, she told him to quit it, and he wouldn't, so she just jabbed with the left, hooked with the right, and that kid went down cold. Never had a problem with Davey Johnson again, unless you count the time last year when I torched his car, but that's another story."

"So how did you know that she was our mom?" Ti asked. "Are you friends with our dad, too?"

"Nah, your dad's a schmuck."

"Hey!" Dixon said, standing up suddenly and angrily, like the Hulk. He backed up so hard into the wall behind him that the chair smashed into pieces. "Nobody inthults my dad!" He ripped open his hands, flinging shards of duct-tape everywhere, grabbed a leg of the chair, and advanced towards Sean. "You take that back you, you, you *poop* head!"

"Calm down, kid," Sean said, backing away and holding the bucket of coffee in front of him for protection. "I was just kidding. I like your dad. I'm sorry what happened. I just didn't take too kindly to the restraining order. We coulda talked it out if he'd just given me the chance."

"You?" Dixon said. "You're the thtalker?"

"Stalking's such an ugly word," Sean said. "And nothing was ever proven in court."

"What's this?" Ti said.

"I remember when I was little, thome creep used to follow our mama around and take pictures of her and ask her to marry him even though she wath already married to dad."

"Hey, I'm an art photographer in my spare time," Sean said, "and she was a work of art." He pulled the can of knock-out spray from his holster and pointed it at Dixon. "Now you better back off, big fella, or you're gonna get a taste of this yourself."

"Down, Dixon," Ti said. "Sit."

Dixon complied, cross-legged on the floor, one of the chair-legs still taped to his enormous calf.

"So here's the deal," Sean said. "I been watchin' you punks rip off my store. And when it was just a little food, I let it slide. I know you're hurtin' like almost everybody else in this crazy town, and a kid's gotta eat. But four hundred and forty three dollars and eleven cents worth of premium fireworks, that's a whole different story. You gonna pay."

"Huh?" said Ti. "I don't understand. The store got the fireworks back."

"Yeah, but now they're blue. So it's real simple," Sean said. "You owe me the money, personal-like, plus my handling fee. We'll call it an even five bills. By the end of the month. Then I erase the security footage, and we're good."

"That's ten days!" Ti said. "We can't!"

"Well you're gonna have ta," Sean said. "Or I turn you over to the Juvies, and you go to the Big House."

"So what's going to happen to the fireworks?" Ti had been hoping they could at least sell them to Parker, since they were paying for them.

"I'm takin' them home myself," Sean said. When he gulped at his coffee bucket again, his head temporarily disappeared from view. "I got this neighbor who's been tickin' me off lately. He lets his dog walk across my lawn."

Chapter 22

The Faber brothers looked for Johnny Fitziguzzi in all of his usual spots. He wasn't in his room, fighting with Doc. He wasn't in the lounge, cheating at cards. He wasn't even in the coffee shop, stealing tips off the tables when the waitresses weren't looking. Where was he?

When they circled back and asked Doc, they figured the old fellow was joking when he bellowed over a re-run of *Desperate Housewives*, "Have you checked the library?"

"What?" Ti yelled back, struggling to hear over the blaring television.

"CHECK. THE. LIBRARY!"

"What?" Ti heard him this time, but could only think of all the times Johnny had told him to stay away from books. "Books make you stupid," Johnny liked to say. "And they cause a thrombosis in your liver. With all the time you save not reading books, you can go to the track and make a little money."

"WHAT, ARE YOU DEAF?" Doc said.

Ti grabbed the remote and hit the mute button. "He's actually in the library?" he said to Doc. "What's he doing there? Burning stuff?"

"You'll see," Doc said, and snatched back the remote. "Now lemme watch my show. That Eva Longoria is about to take a swim."

"He ain't in that place, Brah, I'm tellin' you," Eagle said as they snuck down the nursing-home halls. "Besides, library be shayam!"

Eagle had hated libraries ever since that time when he was eleven and a kindergartener had laughed at him for only reading one book all the time: *The Pokey Little Puppy*. Second of all, he couldn't believe that Johnny Fitziguzzi would ever spend time in such a place unless he'd been kidnapped.

"Let's just check," Ti said. "We've looked everywhere else."

"Have they got cookbookth?" Dixon said. "I need a good recipe for filo."

The nursing home's library was actually more like a closet behind the kitchen, in what had once been a walk-in cooler. There was just one bulb hanging from the ceiling, and shelves along two sides, half-full of fat, yellowed paperbacks. It smelled like rotting leaves.

But there was Johnny. He was sitting on a plastic milk crate, his back to them, smoking a cigar with a white-plastic tip. He was typing so intently on a huge, old computer with a screen the size of a postcard that he didn't notice them.

While Eagle sulked outside the door and Dixon scanned the titles on the shelves for something about Greek cooking, Ti looked over Johnny's shoulder at the tiny screen and read aloud:

"'Chad was a broad shouldered cowboy six feet eleven inches tall with a body like an athlete who turned his movie-star handsome face up to the stars and began to pray. "Please God," he wailed at the almighty heavens, "Make the princess marry me, die of natural causes, and leave me her all her money."'"

Johnny covered the computer's tiny screen with his hands. "What are you doing here?"

"Did you write that yourself, Johnny?" Ti said. "It's so . . . so . . . *psychotic.*"

"Thanks, kid," Johnny said. "Christian romance. It's where the money is these days. Plus, the ladies really go for authors. That Hemingway guy? He was married five times. I figure I finish pounding this out by tomorrow, sell it on Thursday, and I'll be pickin' up my new ride just in time for the weekend. I got my eye on a slightly used Grand Caravan with simulated-wood-grain side panels. That baby is *sharp.*"

Johnny turned around and saw that Dixon and Eagle were there as well. "Oh Christmas, you brought the whole bunch of hooligans, eh? You must want something. What is it? Hurry up. I'm a busy man."

"Well, Mister Fitziguzzi," Ti said sweetly, "we were just wondering if you'd like to buy a turkey-raffle ticket."

"Why should I?"

"Because they pay for Electricity Wednesdays," Ti said.

"I love Electrithity Wednesday," Dixon said, still flipping through the books. "They leave the lightth on all day, tho you can thee thtuff, and in the winter there'th even heat tho the ink doesn't freeze in the pen."

"Yeah, yeah," Johnny said, "I heard that whole sob story before. And I'm behind ya on that one. Back in my day they had electricity in the schools all day, all five days, and they had heat, and they even had a book for every kid."

"Wow," Dixon said. "Books. What'd you do with yourth?"

"Never mind about that," Johnny said. "I'm trying to finish up the next five chapters of this baby in time for lunch. We're having turkey loaf." He didn't actually like eating turkey, but since it made the other inmates sleepy, it was easier for him to go through their purses. "What's in it for me?"

"Well, Mister Fitziguzzi," Ti said, "the winner of the Turkey Raffle gets their own entire turkey. That means they can eat for a week!"

"Don't BS me, kid. I watch the news. I know what happens to the people who win that raffle. You win an entire turkey in this town, people get crazy."

It was true that the last two years' winners had been robbed at knifepoint of their turkeys, but the opportunity to feed their families made most East Westfordians willing to take the risk.

"Please buy one?" Ti said. He held his hands together in front of his chest, as if he was praying. "If we sell the most tickets, we win a valuable prize."

"Oh yeah, right," Johnny said, and spat a wad of cigar slime onto the floor. "Remember last year? They said the winner was gonna get a TV. And what'd they get? They got a *picture* of a TV. Do yourself a favor, kid. Buzz off. You want a prize go rob a store."

This made Eagle perk up. "Okay!"

"No, really," Ti said, pleadingly. "I saw the prize. It's real. A lady from the PTO kept going over to Will Bates' house in North Southington on trash night." Will Bates was the richest man in the state; he'd made billions selling faulty software. "She went through the trash every week for two months, until she found something really good: he was throwing away an IPad 7! And it still works!"

"Big whoopy. Who wants a heating pad?" He hooked a thumb over his shoulder. "I could boost you a dozen off these old folks by tomorrow."

"No, no," Ti explained. "It's not a heating pad. It's a kind of small, portable computer."

"Whata you need a computer for, kid?" Johnny said. "You got no electricity in that bus of yours, so you can't even plug it in. And 'sides, any time you wanna compute something, you can just come over here and use this baby."

He patted the top of the computer, which Ti noticed was made by a company called Mattel. Suddenly the tiny green screen went blank. "Damn!" Johnny said. "There goes my first thirteen chapters!"

"Yo, mang," Eagle said, stepping forward and kneeling down in front of it to take a closer look. "Did you back it up on the floppy?"

"What's a floppy? Some rap gang?"

"No, Brah. It's a prehistoric storage device. A floppy *disc*. It's like, the size of a Frisbee."

"I ain't your Brah, kid," Johnny said, pointing the end of his cigar at him, "and I ain't your bra strap either. Now where's my damned romance?"

"May I?" Eagle said, motioning to the keyboard.

Johnny moved aside. Eagle tapped some keys, clicked the power switch, tapped some more keys, then said, "There you go, Yo. I found most it. Looks like it backed up right to the point where the princess gets tied to the railroad tracks by the evil atheists."

Johnny sighed contentedly. "That's beautiful stuff, ain't it? Just when the train's about to smash her to bits, God comes along and unties the ropes." He relit his stogy with an old Zippo lighter, looked at Ti, and said, "Now then. Where were we?"

"We were hoping you'd buy two hundred tickets, Mister Fitziguzzi. So we can win the prize."

"The prize is crap, kid! Forget about the prize! I'm tellin' ya, you want one a them heating pads, go stick up a hospital or something."

"We don't want it for us," Ti said. "We want it to sell. So we can pay back Castelli."

Ti explained that they owed her $125 by Tuesday, and also another $500 to the security guard, plus 80 pounds of fireworks to Parker.

Johnny seemed disgusted. "You're not really gonna pay her, are you?" he said. "She's a broad."

"She's a broad what can kick your butt, Mang," Eagle said.

Dixon said, "I think she'th dreamy."

"I've crunched the numbers," Ti said, holding up the ancient calculator he kept in his back pocket, "and paying her is actually less than the cost of medical treatment and lost wages after she beats us up."

"Well, I could maybe buy one ticket," Johnny said, "seein' as how I'm about to be a best-seller and all. Would that help?"

"I guess," Ti said, but he dropped his chin, turned his face away from Johnny, covered his eyes with his hands, and made noises as if he was crying. He wasn't actually crying, but this had worked with Johnny countless times before.

"Ah, kid!" Johnny said. "Ah, don't go cryin' on me!" He pulled a yellowed, wrinkled wad of cloth from his pocket that had once been a handkerchief. "Here. Want I should wipe your tears?"

Ti sniffled behind his hands. "No, it's okay."

"Look, kid, you don't need my money to pay this chick. How many tickets you already sold?"

"Fo'ty-fo'," Eagle said. "Jus' like the pistol!"

"So there you go," Johnny said. "You're on your way."

"But that money'th for Electrithity Wednesday!" Dixon said. "Tho we can thee in thchool!"

"Yeah, yeah, well you got bigger problems than that right now. So pocket it. Go sell another 98 tickets or whatever it is, and there ya go. Ya got the broad paid off. Then we'll have this security guard killed."

"But they'll know at the school if we don't pay them," Dixon said. "There's tickets!"

"Lemme see them tickets," Johnny said.

Dixon showed him one, but wouldn't let him touch it.

"Pathetic," Johnny said. "These are easy." He pointed to Eagle. "You. Finish this chapter." He pointed to the computer. "Make the cowboy see some angels or something. And put in some hot chicks. Evil dancin' girls, maybe, in bikinis. Start typin'."

"Tay, Brah!"

"Don't call me that. You two." He pointed at Ti and Dixon. "Come with me."

While Eagle sat down to type, his brothers followed Johnny back to his room.

Doc was now asleep on the bed, his head back and mouth half-open, strange clicking noises coming from his teeth. The television on the wall still blared. A perky woman who seemed like she'd had way too much coffee was smiling and screaming, "I'll buy a vowel!"

Johnny reached under his bed and pulled out an old red-vinyl suitcase. He told the brothers to look away, and covered a tiny padlock with his body while he worked the numbers. Finally, after much cursing, it opened. They heard a zipping noise, then a pause, then more zipping. Then Johnny slid the suitcase back under his bed and yelled, "Okay. Here."

Ti turned to see him offering up a roll of double-sided tickets, exactly like the ones they were using for the Turkey Raffle. "They switched brands over to the Church Carnival, so these are no good to me anymore."

"Thanks, Mister Fitziguzzi!"

Dixon nodded his head in agreement.

Johnny double-checked that Doc was truly asleep by slapping his roommate on the leg. When he didn't move, Johnny slipped his hand under Doc's butt and came out with his wallet.

He opened the wallet, removed a ten-dollar bill, and handed it to Dixon. "Here, kid," he said. "Doc'll says he'll take four tickets, just to get youse started. You can give his change directly to me."

Chapter 23

"I be hungry," Eagle said. "Do you gots the Magic Dollar, Dog?"

Ti stopped walking—they were kicking through the litter on the sidewalk between the Nursing Home and downtown East Westford. He took off his right shoe. This was easy to do, because it was a shiny, lace-up, black-leather adult's shoe he'd borrowed from his father, about four inches longer than his foot. He had stuffed the toes and sides of the shoes with crumpled newspaper and various items important to him. He lifted up the insole, looked inside, and said, "Yup."

"Tha's dope, Brah. Let's hit City Hall."

Dixon and Ti agreed.

There were two rules for successfully using the Magic Dollar to get food: First, they had to find an older-model vending machine. In East Westford that meant most of them, as long as they stayed away from Wally World, the schools, and the bank. Second, they had to find a machine in an area where almost nobody went, so there wouldn't be witnesses. And since the latest round of lay-offs, the most empty place in town was City Hall.

The basement of City Hall had once been a bustling place, with a barber shop, a florist, and a news agent's. Now it was dark, cob-webby, and smelled of cat pee. The only light came from the glow of an old Slice soda machine at the end of the hallway by the bathrooms, which growled and groaned like a diesel engine. To its left was a food-vending machine, and to its right a cigarette machine, now empty, that advertised Winstons and Chesterfields for 75 cents.

"Yummy," Dixon said, as they examined the remaining offerings in the food machine. "They thtill have pork rinds."

"I's gonna have three of them orange Mountain Dews for my appetizer," Eagle said. "That'll get me a bit of a buzz on. Then I'm gonna fill up on the Cheetos."

Ti, who was a very fussy eater, decided on a can of Slice, five packages of Goldfish, and a Three Musketeers for dessert.

"Gimme the Magic Dollar, Brah," Eagle commanded. Ti took off his shoe, pulled it out, and handed it over. Eagle unrolled it. It was a regular green-and-white dollar bill, with long strands of cellophane tape that trailed out of the far end and wrapped around a pencil stub.

Eagle inserted the untaped end into the dollar-reader of the Slice machine, and it registered "1.00" in red numbers on the display. He pressed a button and smiled when a can of soda dropped into the bin at the bottom with a clunk. Then he carefully pulled on the pencil, causing the dollar to re-emerge from the machine. He fed it in again and pressed the button for Ti's Slice. He repeated the process and procured a cranberry juice for Dixon.

Next Eagle fed the dollar into the food-venting machine, and pressed D4. A package of Cheetos dropped down, and a quarter clanged in the change return. He pulled the dollar out again, pressed numbers, and smiled contentedly as bags of food dropped and dimes and quarters fell.

When they were done shopping Ti rolled up the dollar and replaced it inside Ti's shoe. They took their cans and bags of junk and went to sit on the steps of City Hall, where the sun was warm on their faces and they were shielded from the wind by piles of trash-bags higher than their heads. They burped happily and licked cheese dust and grease from their fingers.

When he was done eating, Ti said, "This meeting is called to order. Secretary? Call the roll."

"Oh, shayam, Brah. Do we have to do this?"

"Yes."

"Awright. Dixon?"

"Prethent."

"Ticonderoga?"

"Present."

"Okay, Brah," Eagle said. "We all here."

"You forgot someone," Ti said.

"What?"

"You forgot to call yourself."

"I'm here, Brah. I can see that I'm here."

"You still need to call your name. For the minutes. Otherwise it's not legal."

"Oh come on, Brah!"

"Shall we talk about Fluffy Precious Foofoo?"

"Awright. Eagle? Present. There. We all here. Now get on with it, before we dies of old age."

"Very good," Ti said. "Now then. I would like to discuss the matter of how we are going to pay off our considerable debts. We owe $125 to Castelli by Tuesday, 80 pounds of fireworks to Parker by Friday, and five hundred dollars in cash to that creepy security guard by the end of the month. Questions or comments from the board?"

"The Betty Crocker Bake-Off hath a ten-thousand dollar prize, and I think I could do thomething really extheptional with Warm Delights brownie mix and a jar of Bac-Os."

"Tha's in April, Brah," Eagle said. "We needs the Benjamins to*day*."

"I second Eagle's statement," Ti said. "If we don't satisfy our creditors immediately we will be in deep poop. Any suggestions for speedy fund-raising?"

"I got this, Brah," Eagle said. "We takes that heater you found, and we uses it to stick up the East Westford Savings Bank."

"I vote nay," Ti said. "Remember last month, when Geography Gerry tried that? All he got was two hundred and thirty dollars. And then the attack dogs ripped off his clothes, bit him in the eye, and put him in the hospital. Once they cure the rabies, he's going to jail for six years. The risk-to-earnings ratio is way to high."

Eagle seemed unfazed. He stood up. "Okay, mang. Let's jet. We gonna use your burner to rob da drug dealahs down at the high school. They got loads a scrill."

"Nay," Ti said again. "We've got a little pistol, and they've got machine guns."

"I heard Kingpin Timmy jutht bought a grenade launcher!" Dixon said happily.

"Tay," Eagle said. "I gots more. We'll do like the teachers do when they needs some dead presidents, and have us a bake sale!"

"Oooh," Dixon said. "I can try out my new recipe for bithcotti."

"But we don't have a stove," Ti said.

"I'm building a tholar oven!"

"Will it be completed today?"

"Probably not."

Ti held his calculator. "Some quick math," he said, pecking away at the buttons, "reveals that given the low profit-margin and high spoilage rate of baked goods, if we want to reach our financial goal we'd have to bake and sell three thousand, five hundred and sixteen average-sized chocolate-chip cookies in the next 79 hours, which subtracting shopping, baking, and sleep time means we'd have to sell. . . . 157 cookies per hour, without eating *any* of them ourselves. It can't be done."

"Yeah, but what if they were bithcotti?"

Ti punched more buttons, peered at a number, and said, "Given the low demand in East Westford for any type of luxury coffee-dunking product due to the even lower average income, I predict that biscotti would take us nineteen days. By then Castelli will have broken all our bones."

"Yo, Brah," Eagle said. "Ain't you just little mister negativity."

"Yeah," Dixon said. "If you're tho thmart about bithcotti, why don't you come up with thomething better?"

"I figured you'd ask me that eventually," Ti said. He removed his shoe, took out a little square of paper, and unfolded it on his knee. "So I've taken the liberty of drawing up this plan. Gentlemen, Faber Amalgamated is going into the numbers racket."

"And all the profits from this raffle," Eagle was saying later that day in remarkably understandable language, "will go to help pay for dogs that are suffering from, ah, groundalanoma, which is a horrible disease that affects one in every three labradoodles and causes them to grow, uh, small, green lumps on their ears."

He was speaking to a brown-haired woman in a ball cap and canvas barn coat outside the Happy Hour Liquor Emporium on the west side of town. It was an enormous gray-cement bunker with metal grates over the windows and big cement bollards in the front to stop thieves from smashing their cars through the front doors. She was busily loading cases of vodka from a shopping cart into the back of her rusty Honda Civic. The brothers had noticed a sticker in the window for the North American Labradoodle Association.

"Oh my goodness," the woman said, putting her hand to her chest. "That sounds terrible. What's the prize?"

"The lucky winner," Ti said proudly, "receives a whole turkey every week for a year."

"Oh, no," the woman said. "I wish I could, but I can't."

"Why not, lady?"

"Well," she said nervously, "look what happens to the people who win the Electricity Wednesday turkey raffles for the school. As soon as they get their turkey they get robbed at knifepoint."

"Exactly," Dixon said, waving the little chrome pistol they'd found at the hospital. "Thath why our raffle comes with thith handy hand gun. You can protect yourthelf!"

"I'll take five dollars worth," the woman said reluctantly. She didn't really want to, but the large boy was now pointing a gun at her.

Ti tore five tickets from the roll Johnny Fitziguzzi had given them and handed them over. "Thank you," he said, and bowed slightly. "Have a nice day."

Things had been going okay. Most people said they just couldn't spare a dollar, even though they definitely needed the food and the gun. The brothers said that they understood. But they had told a grandmotherly type wearing an enormous mess of yarn on her head that the money was going to provide knitting needles to homeless children, and she'd bought ten. A young mother bought five tickets after they told her their little sister was dying of beriberi.

They also told a man with a mullet and a blaze-orange vest that the money raised would provide free handguns for white people, and he'd given them a plastic bag of nickels, dimes, pennies, and a freshly killed partridge that he claimed added up to twenty-dollar value. "If you wanna git us back our gun rights, though," he said as he slammed the door of a dark-purple Ford Taurus for the third time, "you're gonna have to blow up the U.N."

And several other people had bought one ticket, just because they liked the idea of weekly meals.

By the time it was too cold and dark to stand outside they'd sold 103 tickets. They used some of the money to buy a pound of meat that hadn't been hit by a car, a bag of potatoes, and also a pound of carrots because Eagle only liked orange food and Dixon was worried about scurvy.

They walked back to the Happy Hour the following morning, but the parking lot was deserted. A cold wind blew plastic bags and beer cans across the weedy pavement. When they asked the old man in the yellow vest whose job it was to round up the shopping carts where all the customers were he looked at them like they were stupid. "What are you, stupid?" he asked. "It's ten in the morning on a Saturday. Ever heard of a hang-over? Things don't start jumpin' around here until after two."

"Crunk," Eagle said to his brothers, disappointed. "We gots to find a different 'hood."

They discussed the various places in East Westford where they could find people who weren't poor and who went outside, none of them good. There was the parking lot at Wally World, but they were afraid of that crazy little security guard—they all still had bits of blue paint behind their ears and under their fingernails. There were always big crowds of people outside the Soup Kitchen, but those folks didn't have any money. And whenever non-customers like them went anywhere near the bank, the guards smacked them on the backs of their legs with bamboo rods that really, really hurt.

Dixon suggested they go back to their bus, warm up, and cook some potatoes. His brothers agreed. As they approached the lot, however, they heard loud noises coming from the other side of the Brimmingham Academy fence: air horns, vuvuzelas, amplified music, even shotgun fire.

"Yo, Brahs," Eagle said. "Somepin goin' on today at the Brim. Who wants to go check it?"

"I do," Dixon said. "I thmell grilled chicken."

Ti said, "Bring the tickets."

Down the tunnel, under the fence, up through the former gardening barn, around the security guards, behind the bushes, they crept towards the sound, until they found a large party going on in the parking lot in front of the Chip S. and Muffy H. Rand Memorial Football Arena. They could see an *a capella* group on a stage surrounded by walls of speakers, just finishing up a song in multiple harmonies that contained the words, "For you can't out-drink a Brimmingham Guy . . . With his scotch and his bourbon and his whiskey dry. And gin."

Beyond the stage they could see heated tents with clear plastic sides, and servers standing behind outdoor buffet tables covered with steaming trays of food. Beyond the meat-covered grills, they could see hoards of well-dressed people dancing, milling about, drinking heavily, and occasionally falling down. Over in the sandbox, a boy in a blue blazer who looked to be about Ti's age finished off the contents of a green glass bottle, tossed it over his shoulder, flapped his arms, screeched like a crow, and ran around awkwardly screaming, "I'm a bird!"

One night after they'd visited Parker, Dixon had instinctively checked the contents of the trashcans behind Parker's dorm. There he had found, in addition to three china plates, two silver spoons, and an unopened can of Annie's P'sketti-Os, an extra-large, green-and-burgundy, hooded sweatshirt lined with llama fur, the Brimmingham Academy logo embossed on the front in antique gold script. And there was absolutely nothing wrong with it. He'd been wearing it ever since.

As the three brothers stood in a cluster of rhododendron bushes on the outskirts of the parking lot, watching a fistfight between two old men and inhaling the luscious scent of roasting steaks and frying potatoes, a balding young man with tufts of blonde hair, his face painted green on one side and burgundy on the other, staggered towards them and dropped the bottle of champagne he'd been carrying. He stepped behind a nearby shrub, unzipped his jeans, and began to pee.

Meanwhile, assuming from his sweatshirt that Dixon was a fellow alum, the drunken man said to him, "Ciao, Brimmy!"

"Hello," Dixon replied tentatively.

The man's voice was slurred, as if he had water in his mouth. "Should be a smashing victory for the old prep today, don't you think?"

Dixon grunted. He wanted to run away.

The man zipped up and faced them. "Those fifth-years they've recruited are simply enormous, aren't they?"

Dixon nodded again.

"Say," the man said to him, pointing a wobbly finger at the three brothers, "If the five of your are done vomiting in the bushes, you really ought to try the smoked salmon at the Class of '83 tent. Binks Buffington had it flown in from Alaska this morning on one of his jets, and it is exquisite."

"Okay," Dixon said, and made a bee-line for one of the tents. The thought of eating seafood had overpowered his fear.

Now Ti stepped up to the drunk and smiled charmingly. "Would you like to buy some lottery tickets, sir? The money raised goes to provide, uh, smoked salmon to fifth-years."

The man's head wobbled for a while like a bobble-head, but gradually he seemed to focus on the small boy in front of him. "Do I know you?"

"Oh, *yes*," Ti said.

"Where do you come from?"

Ti tried to think of an answer that sounded rich. "Uh, Chutney."

"Chutney?" the man said. "Do you mean Alexandra Chutney? Of the Tuxedo Park, New York, Chutneys?"

"Uh, *yes!*" Ti said. "That's it."

"But she's ninety-seven years old, my dear boy," the man said, rubbery on his legs. "She's been dead for three years."

The man wasn't making sense, so Ti just nodded and said, "That's right."

"And I've never met her."

"Maybe it was through her grandson," Ti suggested.

"But he was killed in the Boer War, by a damned Bolshevik!" The drunken man removed his sunglasses, leaned down, and examined Ti's face closely. His breath smelled like the empty liquor bottles at school. "Hold on a minute. I don't know you. And you've got blue paint behind your ears. Blue! The color of our sworn enemy. You're not a Brimmy, are you? You're a damned accursed Halberdinck in disguise!" He took two floppy steps back, pointed a finger at Ti, and yelled, "Guards! Arrest this man! He's a Halberdinck spy!"

"Run for it," Ti said to Eagle. Just then, however, a strong hand grabbled each of them by the back of the neck. They couldn't move.

Chapter 24

"Halberdincks, you say?" said the voice behind them, which appeared to belong with the hands that held them tight. "On the Brimmy side? Kneel!" The hands pushed Eagle and Ti face-down to the ground.

"You know what that calls for, don't you?" the voice said. It had an odd kind of German-English-Russian accent, "We vill haff to give them the old Brimmy Ride."

"Oh lets," said the drunken man excitedly. He leaned in towards Ti and said, "We're going strip you, paint you with tar, fill your bellies with the cheapest brand of vodka available, paddle your bottoms with the Icky Stick until you're black and blue, then leave you in the middle of a highway tied to a tricycle. It's such fun!"

"But before that," said the voice. "Let us make them do the Donkey Walk."

"Absolutely," the drunken man slurred. "It's utterly humiliating. And perhaps a few hours of the Flaming Dogey."

"That can be fatal," the voice said.

"I know!" said the drunken man. "Won't it be extraordinary?"

"Please sir!" Ti pleaded. "This is all a giant misunderstanding. I'm not a Halberdinck. It's not my fault! I . . . I . . ." He tried to think of something. "I was kidnapped."

"Kidnapped, you say?" said the drunk.

"Yeah, that's it!" Eagle whined. "We was kidnapped by the Halberwhatevahs, and painted blue, and then they wiped off the blue, and we was tied up and put in a van, and the van drove us to the middle of nowhere, and then it was the . . . uh . . ."

"It was the French!" Ti tossed out.

"The French?" demanded the drunk.

"Yeah, the French!" Eagle said.

"Those snail-eating communists," the drunk said. "I hate the French."

There was a pause, during which time the brothers could hear the heavy breathing of the person who held them down, and in the distance the *a capella* group singing something about the evils of regulation.

Finally the drunk slurred, "But we're still going to humiliate them, right?"

"Absolutely," said the voice. "First, however, I vood like to interview them in private. If you'll excuse me?"

"Surely," said the drunk, and picked up the champagne bottle he'd dropped. "Say, this shampers is still good!"

The voice said, "Stand, vermin!"

When they did, the hands dragged them backwards into the bushes and tossed them to the ground. Eagle and Ti turned their heads to see that the voice belonged to Parker Worthington, dressed today in an enormous fur coat.

The brothers stood up and brushed the perfect blades of Brimmingham grass from their clothes while Parker stared at them.

Then, in his normal voice, he said, "You two are running some sort of poor person's swindle, aren't you?"

"No!" Ti said.

"Then kindly explain this!" Parker held out the roll of tickets.

"We found them, Brah," Eagle said.

"Nonsense. I suspect you're taking advantage of the drunken state of my Brimmingham comrades to sell them bogus shares in some spurious game of chance."

"No way, Homey! We clean!"

"Tell me the truth," Parker said, leaning in very close to Ti, "or I will be forced to alert our security forces. *And.* I'll take back my platinum access card."

Ti told him the truth.

When he was done Parker crossed his furry arms over his chest and said, "I get twenty percent."

"Five," Ti said.

"Ten," Parker said.

"Deal." Ti held out his small hand, and they shook on it.

Parker, all smiles now, led the brothers back to the drunken man, who was lying on his back and peering down the top of the champagne bottle, his green and burgundy face-paint now smeared on one side.

"G. Newton Norquist," Parker said to the drunken man, "This has been a wonderful prank, hasn't it? But enough with the high-jinx. Now I'd like you to meet the Faber brothers. They are raising money for a worthwhile charity through the sales of tickets. May I count you in for a hundred?"

The man called Newt said, "What the hell." He rolled over onto his stomach and with some difficulty removed a wallet from the back pocket of his jeans.

"And I'm giving very good odds that Brimmingham will beat Halberdincks today. 14 to one. Would you care to place a small wager?"

Newt sat up. He pulled all the bills from his wallet, threw them up in the air, and giggled. "Five hundred on Brimmy," he slurred.

Parker gathered up the bills, handed two fifties to Ti, and pocketed the rest.

Ti tore off a long chain of lottery tickets and handed them to Newt, but he didn't seem to see them. "I'm all out of shampers," he said, and with Parker's help he stood up. He waved an index finger in their general direction and said, "I'll see you four over at the bar." Then, eyes fixed on the champagne tent, G. Newton Norquist staggered off.

"Lovely man," Parker said as they watched him go. "Didn't even ask about the point-spread. It's Brimmingham by 49."

"I don't understand," Ti said. "What is all this? How 'come everybody's drunk in the morning, and they're not even poor?"

Parker laid a friendly hand on his and Eagle's shoulders, and pointed them towards the food tables. "Homecoming, my dear boys," he explained. "They're intoxicated not to drown their economic sorrows, as your people might, but in celebration of the big game today: our mighty rivalry of the gridiron."

"Huh?"

"Football! Brimmingham and Halberdincks have battled it out with the old pigskin since 1879. It's tradition!"

"And what's a point spread?"

As they filled their plates with crab cakes, lobster tails, and bacon-wrapped duck breasts, Parker explained to them the ways of prep-school football. He said that Brimmingham rarely had enough students willing to engage in such injury-prone sports as football—too much of that dangerous tackling, hitting, and falling down. So they offered scholarships to twenty or thirty "fifth-year students," top players from around the world who were happy to spend a year here, eating good food and forever claiming on their resumes that they had graduated from such an elite institution.

"This year we've got seven linemen who used to play in the NFL," Parker explained, "as well as quite a few of those people whose job it is to catch the ball. Brimmingham ought to do quite magnificently, but Humberdinck has half the former team from Penn State, so it will shine as well. And as long as Brimmingham wins by less than 49—something I've insured by making healthy *donations* to several of our key players—I should make out quite handsomely. Now then; hurry up. There's not much time before the match begins. And don't forget about my fireworks. I've just received word that Phillie Phanatic, who is some sort of important athletics celebrity, will be in attendance at my party for Francisco Antonia."

While Dixon continued to gorge on sushi, tomato juice, and T-bone steak at a table in one of the heated tents, Ti and Eagle worked the crowd. They told a young blonde woman in jodhpurs and riding boots that the prize for their raffle was the new Range Rover Mega Savannah SUV, and that all the proceeds were going to combat climate change. "Awesome," she said. "I'm all about the environment. And I really need a bigger SUV." She handed over a hundred-dollar bill.

They told a pale, doughy faced old man in a blue blazer and a Brimmingham tie that the the proceeds would benefit the Class Fairness Super Pac, which was working to eradicate taxes for millionaires. He pulled a thick wad of bills from the pocket of his flannels, removed the gold clip, and peeled off three crisp 50s.

Another woman, dressed in a pink sweater and bright green pants embroidered with tennis racquets, nearly cried when Ti described their alleged work to rescue outdated sailing yachts. By the time servants in white gloves had wandered through the crowds ringing silver bells to announce the start of the game, the Faber brothers had accumulated a thick stack of bills.

"That was easy," Ti said as they watched the crowds stagger into the stadium, from which they now heard cheers, gunfire, screaming, and the music of marching bands.

"Yeah," Dixon said, gnawing meat off a giant beef rib. "You can jutht take whatever you want, and they don't even charge money. Help me fill up a garbage bag with the oysterth. And grab that bottle of Bordeaux. It'll make an excellent thauce."

Chapter 25

An hour later, Ti sat behind his little cardboard-box desk in their "office" under the bus, counting the stack of bills yet again. Ever since they had left Brimmingham Academy, Dixon had been describing the great dinner he was going to cook them tonight. "Then I'm gonna buy thome curry powder," he said, "and blend it with a bit of yoghurt, and make chicken tandoori. You're gonna love it. I've had chicken before, and it tastes way better than pigeon."

Ti placed the last green bill neatly on his stack, squared it up with the palms of his hands, and said, "Yup, that's the fifth time I've counted it, and it still comes out to 937 dollars. We can pay off everybody and still have money left over for allergy pills and food."

Eagle had been lounging in a corner of the office, flipping longingly through an old puppy calendar. Suddenly he perked up. "Yo Brah, did you say nine hundred?"

"Yes I did. Nine hundred and thirty-seven, to be exact."

"Nine hundred is what M.C. Larry charges for the Premium Pack Platinum Plan!"

"No!" Ti said. "We need to pay off our debts."

"We *can*, Brah," Eagle said. "The Premium Pack Platinum Plan is guaranteed to triple our money!"

"It's guaranteed to *lose* our money," Ti said. "M.C. Larry is an idiot."

"Yeth he ith," Dixon agreed. "Remember that time he tried to cook a chicken inthide a clothes drier?"

"Doink!" Eagle yelled, grabbed the pile of cash, and slithered out the opening into the light. They could see the back of him, running through the weeds and abandoned appliances to the street.

"Dixon!" Ti said. "Go get him!"

"No!"

"Why not? He's running away with our money."

"Because whenever I thtand up in here I bump my head on the bottom of the buth, and it gives me an ouchy!"

"Dixon," Ti said very calmly, "if Eagle gives that money to M.C. Larry, there will be no money left over for tandoori."

"Thuperman to the rescue!" Dixon yelled. His hands in fists, he tried to jump up into a crime-fighting posture. Instead he bumped his knuckles on a piece of muffler. He sat down, rubbed his hand, then crawled out from under the bus and lumbered off.

A few minutes later, Eagle was seated on a yellow plastic chair in the Suds-O-Mat, facing M.C. Larry and eating a bag of sour-cream-and-onion potato chips. The place was hot and steamy and smelled like the cheap perfume of a thousand drier sheets.

A smallish man in his late fifties, M.C. Larry managed the place, and claimed to have recording studio in the basement. He had a Rhode Island accent, a big head of unnaturally dark, molded hair, long sideburns, and a handlebar mustache. He was wearing a forest of chains around his neck, sunglasses with lenses the size of softballs, and a mustard-colored track suit.

He sat behind the folding card table that served as his desk at the back of the Suds-O-Mat. On either side of him stood two dark-haired boys, also dressed in track suits, who he was introducing to Eagle. "These ah my sons, M.C. Larry Junior and M.C. Frankie Junior."

"If he's your son," Eagle said, pointing to the older one, "how 'come he's called *Frankie* Junior?"

"I dunno," M.C. Larry said, taking a swig from a big bottle of malt liquor. "Ask his mother."

"Well anyhow, Brah," Eagle said, "I wants me the Premium Pack Platinum Plan. Thas the one with the laser lights and the super-sub woofers and the dancin' girls, right? My first hit album's gonna be called Rap Supa Cool Dope."

"Sure, kid," M.C. Larry said. "Just gimme the nine large and we'll go down the cellah an' get started right now."

Eagle reached into the pocket of his baggy jeans, pulled out the wad of cash, and had just handed it over the table to M.C. Larry when they heard a boy scream above the roar of the washers and driers, "No!"

Eagle turned and saw his brothers. He held up the bag of chips and said to them, "But look what M.C. Larry gave me! He has his own vending machine!"

"Wow," Dixon said. "Doeth it have jalapeño cheese crackerth too?"

"Dixon," Ti barked. "Tandoori chicken."

"Oh yeah!" Dixon sprinted around the top-loading washers and the change-making machine and dove towards M.C. Larry, his hand outstretched. He grabbed the stack of money with one hand and shoved M.C. Larry's chest with the other, causing M.C. Larry to fall backwards onto the linoleum. As soon as he got back up he patted his head and readjusted his hair.

Eagle had wrapped both of his hands around Dixon's much larger hands, which completely covered the wad of bills. "Gimme that green, Brah!" he shrieked. "Thas for my supa-dope rap!"

"No," Dixon said. "It'th for tandoori." With a quick super-hero move he kicked Eagle in the stomach, knocking him into the laundry-soap dispenser. Eagle got back up and ran towards him, but at the exact moment Ti stuck out his giant dress-shoe, tripping him. Eagle's head slammed into a drier.

When Eagle stood up again, Dixon grabbed him by either side of his baggy jeans and lifted him so high up that his shiny gold basketball sneakers wiggled six inches above the floor.

Still Eagle wouldn't give up: He yelled "Hand kick!" and punched Dixon in the face.

This hurt Eagle's hand more than Dixon's jaw, but now the older brother was annoyed. Noticing an open top-load washer in the row in front of him, he carried Eagle over, still suspended by his pants and smacking at Dixon's head, and tipped Eagle head-first into the machine.

Ti and Dixon stood there, panting and giggling at the way Eagle's feet flopped in the air, until they heard a high, scary voice behind them.

"Freeze, punks!"

They turned to see Larry Junior, the younger son, standing behind them, holding a pipe wrench over his head. It was nearly as big as he was, and so heavy that even though he held it with both hands it wobbled in the air, threatening to fall down and crush their toes.

"You made a deal," Larry Junior squawked. "You ordered the Premium Pack Platinum Plan, complete with the laser lights, the super sub woofers, and the dancing girls. So hand over the money or I'll brain ya with this!"

Ti just smiled, his right hand in his pants pocket. He removed the little silver gun they'd found at the hospital, pointed it at the other boy, and said, "you put that down or I'll brain *you* with this. Who do you think would win?"

"I'll put ten bucks on the gun," M.C. Larry said. "Them are way faster."

Chapter 26

Dixon had just pulled Eagle by the wrist through the automatic doors of Wally World when somebody screamed at them, "Freeze, suckahs!"

A short man with a buzz-cut jumped out from behind the shopping carts and pointed a huge can of pepper spray at them. It was Sean. He was wearing his usual bright-orange security-guard uniform, with a holster around his waist. One pocket of the holster was now empty. In the other they could see a big can of blue spray-paint.

"I knew you'd come back here eventually," Sean said rapidly, his left hand over the can of spray paint, his eyebrows wiggling up and down like ocean waves on a windy day. "You wanna boost some more of my stuff, don't you?"

"No sir," Ti said sweetly, smiling up at the man. "We've come here to repay you."

"And to buy curry powder!" Dixon said excitedly.

"Oh yeah?" Sean said suspiciously. "Show me the money."

"Here?" Ti asked. "Wouldn't it be safer in your office? It's a lot of money."

"Right," Sean said. "Good idea, kid. Follow me."

He lead them through the full-body scanner and around the corner past the bathrooms. He swiped a card, and a thick metal door automatically opened. They followed him into a small lobby and towards a metal grate. He made them close their eyes while he looked at some numbers he'd written on the palm of his hand and punched them, one at a time, into a keypad on the wall. The grate split in half and receded into the walls.

They walked for quite a while down a long, carpeted hallway with locked doors on both sides that smelled like air freshener. Eventually they stopped. Sean climbed up a ladder on the wall and unlocked a hatch in the ceiling with a brass key the size of Hershey bar. When he was up on the floor above he gestured for them to follow.

At the top of the ladder the brothers found themselves in another carpeted hallway the same as the one they'd left. This time, however, they walked to the right for what seemed like about a mile, until they turned left, then right, then straight ahead to the end. They now faced a thin wooden door like the sort they'd seen in their friend Biff's trailer. It was labeled with big yellow letters, "Security Center. Keep Out. Authorized Personnel Only. Do Not Read This Sign Without Permission."

In the middle of the door, orange letters scrolled across the screen of a glowing green box that read "Place hand on scanner."

Sean put his right hand onto the face of the box and waited. The box glowed brighter, made whizzing and popping noises, then stopped. New words scrolled across its screen: "Denied."

"Krikey," Sean said. "Not this again."

He waited until the machine had reset and the orange letters instructed him to place his hand on the scanner again, wiped his hand on the side of his pants, and placed it on the screen.

Again the machine glowed, whizzed, and popped, and again he was denied.

This time he spit on his fingers and rubbed them on his shirt. Still the door wouldn't open.

He tried it two more times.

Finally he'd had enough. He pounded his fist on the door. The flimsy door cracked slightly and swung open.

Sean flicked on the light switch, removed his holster, and hung it up on a hook behind the door. He sat down in his swivel chair in front of the banks of screens, opened the mini-fridge by his feet, and pulled out a can of Starbucks Espresso Fortissimo.

"Who wants one?"

It smelled good. Eagle tried to raise his hand, but Dixon kicked him. "That's loaded with thodium gluterate," he hissed. "What are you, thilly?"

Sean shrugged. "Suit yourself." He pointed to the big pill-dispenser on the wall. "No- Doze?"

"No."

"Well I'll do one, just to take the edge off." He cracked open the pop-top, pressed down the dispenser lever, took a pill, and washed it down with a big swig from the can. "Okay. Let's get down to business."

Ti bent down, removed his shoe, and took out an envelope from inside. He stood and held the envelope in front of him. "Five hundred dollars," he said.

"Gimme that."

Sean grabbed at the envelope, but Ti pulled it away. "Remember? You agreed to erase the security tapes."

"Sure, sure," Sean said, the side of his mouth twitching. "Got 'em right here." He stood, went to an old green filing cabinet in the corner, unlocked the middle drawer with a key, and removed a disc. "Here you go, kid," he said. "Now hand over the dough."

Ti examined the disc, then gave it to Eagle. "Is this the only copy?"

"Sure kid, sure," Sean said. "Come on now. I got stuff to do."

With his free hand, Ti pulled the handgun from the waistband of his pants and pointed it at Sean. "Eagle," he said. "Check the hard drive, the back up, and the cloud."

While Dixon grabbed the pepper spray and paint canisters from the holster and pointed them at Sean, Eagle knelt in front of the computer console, tapped some keys, and began searching. "Yo, mang!" he said after a few minutes. "Here we be!"

Three grainy videos appeared on the screens that showed them shoplifting Sugar Booms, chocolate truffles, and fireworks.

"Look at me!" Eagle said. "I look dope!"

"You tried to deceive us, Sergeant Schultz, didn't you?"

"What?" Sean said. "Me? Never. Musta been some kind of mistake."

"Woah, homey," Eagle said after awhile. "You got copies of this crunk all over the place. I'ma just torch the whole dang system."

"No!" Sean yelled and jumped at him, but first Dixon gave him a shot of pepper spray in the eyes, followed by a few spritzes of blue paint. Sean grabbed at his face, fell to the floor, and wailed.

"Ith that made with habeñero, would you say?" Dixon said, sniffing the fiery smell in the air. "Or more of an Ancho chili?"

Eagle clicked a few more keys. The lights in the room dimmed for a second, then the entire console in front of him went black. Eagle smiled contentedly. Then he had an idea: He grabbed the microphone mounted in the middle of the console, clicked it on, and said, "Attention, Wally World shoppers! The security system is currently down. Help yo'selves!"

"I think that concludes our business here," Ti said, and dropped the envelope of money on Sean's squirming chest. "Have a nice day!"

Chapter 27

The Faber brothers wheeled their shopping carts out of Wally World through a crowd of happy people. They passed a chubby old lady carrying a flat-screen TV that was bigger than she was. Beside her, small children were ripping open enormous plastic bags of frosted marshmallows, and a hairy man with low-hanging shorts that revealed thong underwear struggled under the weight of an Alpine Rock Waterfall Fountain, recently price-hacked to $599.

"Why we doin' this, Brah?" Eagle whined. They were each pushing a cart, which between the three of them contained 52 frozen turkey breasts, 86 pounds of fireworks, and all the fixings for a delicious dinner.

Ti said, "Because it's the right thing to do."

Eagle stopped pushing and stood in his way. "But we *banditos*! We don't gots to do the right thing."

"In the immortal words of Bob Dylan," Ti countered, "'To live outside the law you must be honest.' We promised the winner a turkey a week and a handgun, and that's what we're going to deliver. Now move it!"

"Jeeze, Brah," Eagle said. "In the immortal words of a bumper-sticker I saw last week, You needs to wag more and bark less."

"I can't wag," Ti said. "I don't have a tail."

"If you was a dog you could wag," Eagle said.

"But I'm not a dog."

"It would be better if you was a dog. Tha's one more reason why dogs is better than kids. Dogs ain't always tellin' you what to do. Draw that up for me, will ya Dixon?"

"Thure."

That morning, at Ti's insistence, the brothers had placed all the ticket stubs their lottery customers had filled out into a plastic shopping bag. Then they had asked their father to reach in and select one. The winning ticket bore the name of a man named Dimitri Gerbatov, who lived in room 13G of the Sunset Apartments on Boulevard Street. They now trudged up three flights of stairs with the turkeys—it took them five trips—and left

Dixon downstairs in the lobby to guard the remaining contents of their carts.

Eagle knocked on a door labeled 13G. It was made of reinforced metal with a peephole in the middle, painted a bright, drippy red. They heard a scurrying inside, then the sound of something heavy being dragged over a floor, then a slight bang suggesting it had been pushed up against the inside of the door. Then silence.

They waited for a while.

Nothing.

Eagle knocked again.

Silence.

Finally Eagle pounded his fist on the door, and Ti called out in his sweet, high-pitched voice, "Mister Gerbatov!"

The peephole changed colors, from white to dark brown, as if someone was looking at them.

A voice from inside with a thick accent said, "Why you here? What you want? Is not Halloveen!"

"You're the lucky winner!" Ti yelled through the door.

"Win what?"

"The Turkey Raffle."

"What is this thing?"

"From in front of the Happy Hour Liquor Emporium, on Friday. You bought the winning ticket!"

"I bought ticket? I give you dollar because I think is required by government."

"No way, Mang," Eagle said. "You gets to eat good tonight. You won the turkey!"

"I win prize?"

"Yes, sir."

"Slide under door."

"But it's a turkey. It won't fit."

"Leave in mail box."

"There's fifty-two!"

"Who sent you? This is trick to make me open door."

"No sir," Ti said calmly, and held up one of the frozen turkey breasts so the man could see it through the peephole. "This is yours. We just want to give it to you."

"Okay," the man said. "I will open door leetle bit. But I warn you. I have gun!"

After a while they heard the heavy object pushed across the floor again, then keys jingling on the other side of the door, then locks clicking and bolts sliding. The door opened about three inches, held in place by a chain at the top and another at the bottom. They could see the sliver of a large man peering out at them. He was wearing a tight, red-plastic shirt that barely covered his big belly.

"Okay," he said. "Give me prize."

Eagle held up one of the turkey breasts and tried to shove it through the crack in the opening, but it wouldn't fit.

"Please sir," Ti said, sounding as if he was about to cry. "If you'll just open your door we won't be long. They're really heavy."

"You come alone?"

"Yes."

"You swear?"

"We swears to God, Brah."

"I am atheist."

"We swears to Clint Eastwood, then."

"Okay. I trust Eastwood. I open door."

He closed it again, removed the remaining chains, and re-opened it. The inside of the room smelled like cleaning products. It was immaculate, but all the walls, the kitchen table, the chairs, the little sink and stove, even the ceiling had been painted bright red. The windows were covered with plywood. The only light came from a buzzing florescent fixture in the middle of the ceiling.

When the brothers had finished piling all 52 of the frozen turkey breasts on his red-shag rug, they handed the man the final part of his prize: the handgun.

He tossed the gun on the table, held up one of the turkey breasts, and growled at them, "Where is rest of bird?"

"Tha's the best part, Brah!" Eagle said. "The breast! It's tender and juicy, with a little pop-up button to tell you when it's done!"

"I'm sorry sir," Ti said. "But we couldn't fit enough of the whole ones in our carts."

"But you tell me I win turkey. This not turkey. This part of turkey."

Ti turned on his about-to-cry voice. "But there's 52!"

"Yes," said the man, "and where I to keep 52 turkey?" He swept his arm around the room. "Do you see giant block of ice?"

"Hey, Brah," Eagle said, as he and Ti backed quickly out the door. "Ain't no security right now at Wally World. Why don't you go down there and boost yourself a chest freezer?"

As the brothers walked along the side of the Interstate, it started to rain. This was the quickest way to the Hovering Parents Cooperative Community Charter School, since Johnny Fitziguzzi had refused to loan them his electric wheelchair. As cars buzzed past them at 70 and 80 miles an hour honking their horns, water flew up from the tires and soaked the parts of them that weren't already wet. It was dark and cold, and they were shivering.

Suddenly a particularly loud car vroomed past—a vintage green Porsche convertible. Rather than disappear up the highway, however, it slammed its brakes, making the tires squeal and smoke. The tail lights of the cars behind it lit up like red neon. They honked and veered around the green sportscar.

The brothers heard the Porsche's gears grind and its tires squeal again: The car was backing up, the wrong way on the interstate, coming towards them.

They turned and ran, but the Porsche screeched to a halt beside them. The driver's window came down an inch. "Get in the back," a gruff voiced yelled, "or I'll break your feet."

When the brothers complied, the doors automatically locked.

They were now looking at the back of the driver's head, which had black hair under a knitted cap. Cars flew past them on the right side, honking, swerving, water splashing against the doors. The driver didn't seem to care.

Eventually the head turned. It was Castelli.

"Are you old enough to drive?" Dixon asked.

"No."

"Snorky!" Eagle said.

Castelli shook a black-leather fist at them and said, "I want my money."

"We have it for you right here," Ti said, patting his enormous shoe. "But can you please pull over to the shoulder? We could get killed."

She flicked open a switchblade and pointed it at him. "If you don't give me my money by tomorrow night," Castelli said, "I'm gonna carve my initials on your butt."

"Yo, Briz!" Eagle said. "We gots the green! We gots it right here. We's here to pay you!"

"Then when I'm done with that," she continued, seeming not to hear them, "I'm gonna take *these*," she held up three shiny, sharp, ninja throwing stars, "and use you for target practice."

"Oh most beautiful goddeth!" Dixon said. "More amazing than Batgirl! Hear our plea! We have come to honor you with all the money we owe you!"

"Shut up, giant boy," Castelli growled. "Then after I've filled you up like a pin cushion, I'm going to use this!" She brandished a shiny chrome device with a sharp needle on top. "I'm going to tattoo your faces with unicorns and rainbows!"

By now Ti had taken the wet envelope of cash from his shoe and removed the bills. He held it up in front of her face and said sweetly, "This is for you. It's money!"

"Oh."

"And we'll pay you another fifty," Ti said, "if you drive us home. Our groceries are getting soaked."

When the Porsche screeched to a stop in front of the Faber's old bus, the rain had stopped, and the sky in the west had turned a beautiful shade of pinkish, orangish red.

"Would you like to come in for an appetizer, O goddeth woman?" Dixon said nervously. "I'm preparing chicken tandoori tonight."

To all of their surprise, Castelli said, "What the hell. Why not?"

Inside the bus, their father sat up in his bed and said hello. When he began to sneeze, Dixon handed him a box of tissues, a special treat they'd brought him. "Father," Dixon said, introducing him to Castelli, "I'd like you to meet my future wife."

"It's a pleasure," Mr. Faber said, and reached out his hand.

"Don't count on it," snarled Castelli in Dixon's direction, but she seemed slightly amused.

As she extended her arm to return his handshake, Mr. Faber noticed something on the girl's forearm. Amazed, he studied her face closely.

"What ith it, Father?" Dixon asked.

Mr Faber was still holding Castelli's hand in his. He turned it to reveal the small, elegant tattoo of a crown on her wrist. "May I ask, young lady," he said, both polite and agitated, "where you got that amazing tattoo?"

"I don't know," Castelli growled, pulling her arm back. "I have to go." She pushed past Dixon and rushed out of the bus.

Chapter 28

"What is this, a stag party?" Johnny Fitziguzzi said. When he had walked up the steps into their bus and seen only the Faber brothers and their father, he had seemed disappointed. "If I'd known there was only gonna be you bucks here I woulda found a couple a chorus girls. Instead all I brought was this old fart." He hooked a thumb over his shoulder at his roommate, Doc, who was all dressed up tonight in a leisure suit, his hair fluffed into a big grey Afro. "I had to bring him, or he'd turn me in to the nurses."

"Ith not a thtag party, Mister Fitziguzzi," Dixon said from his kitchen area around the stove. "Ith a dinner party. We bought *food!*"

"Our debts are paid off," Ti said proudly, "and now whenever we run out of food we know how to earn more money to buy more food: by selling more lottery tickets. Now we can eat dinner every night!"

Doc said, "I smell beef cooking. I haven't seen actual beef in years."

"If it's a stag party," Johnny said, looking around at the decorations, "It must be a stag party for a bunch of girly men."

While they'd been gathering up the ingredients for this celebration at Wally World, Dixon had seen a large box labeled "Extra Jumbo Party Kit," and had tossed it into his cart. When he'd opened it up back in the bus, however, he'd discovered that it wasn't the makings of just any kind of party; it was for an enormous Little Mermaid party. Now the bus was decorated with dozens of pink balloons, crepe-paper streamers, a banner reading "Happy Birthday," even a mermaid piñata. The board where they ate now sported a pink-and-purple plastic tablecloth, plates, cups, and party favors. There were no lights on in the bus except for candles. It smelled of chocolate, cinnamon, and French fries.

Christine and Gordo, who were sculptors and Ti's godparents, arrived next, with several bottles of homemade beer. Aunt Patty and her new girlfriend Padme brought a pitcher of margaritas and a box of cupcakes. Mister Faber, thanks to the allergy pills and decongestants they'd gotten him at Wally World, was also sitting upright at the head of the table, sneeze-free. He still looked a little pale, but he was smiling and telling a story about a delivery person at the pencil factory who was pathologically afraid of Morris dancers. This made the adults laugh.

Dixon served them an amazing series of dishes on the pink-paper Mermaid plates: An appetizer of Pasta Carbonara, then salmon sashimi, then filets of beef with a red wine sauce, a Caesar salad, and milkshakes for dessert.

More people came by, and he made them milkshakes too: Ti's friend Maeve, a little Salvadorian girl with chocolate skin and long, curly black hair; Eagle's buddy Waldo, and his family; a tall, thin blonde woman named Anna who looked like a super-model, with her equally tall brother. Dixon had met Anna in the swamp by the river where they both liked to trap food. Even M.C. Larry showed up with Frankie Junior and Larry Junior and a package of hot dogs.

After dinner Mr. Faber made a short speech of thanks to his sons for the medicine and the meal. "I've given you almost nothing," he said, his eyes growing shiny, "and you've given me everything." The crowd clapped.

Next Eagle blind-folded Ti and allowed him the first whack at the Little Mermaid piñata hanging from the bus's ceiling. Ti flailed around, whacking a bed and the stove pipe and a piece of the window. Eagle's, Dixon's, Maeve's and Waldo's turns didn't go much better.

Finally Johnny Fitziguzzi tossed aside the bottle of wine he'd finished and yelled, "You kids are pathetic. When I was your age I was winning cage fights." He grabbled the bat.

Besides the wine, Johnny had also consumed home-brewed beer and several of Mr. Faber's allergy pills, so he was loose on his feet. After Eagle had tied the pink blindfold around his head, Johnny smashed wildly with the plastic bat, hitting Gordo in the thigh, knocking down Ti's book shelf, then connecting like Babe Ruth with the side of the table. It tipped off its base of milk crates. Cups, plates, plastic utensils, and food slid onto the guests and the floor of the bus.

Johnny ripped off the blindfold to see what the noise and shouts of pain were all about. Then he growled "To hell with it," and went after the piñata in earnest. A few good hits and it fell to the floor, where he shoved the shiny black heel of his shoe into the mermaid's head. "There you go!" he said, and collapsed triumphant on a bed. *"That's* how it's done."

The kids moved instinctively to the candy and trinkets that spilled out, but Dixon got there first, boxed them out with his big body, and held up his hand like a traffic cop. "Thtop!" he said. "They could be toxic!"

While the other kids crowded around him, Dixon picked through the lollipops, gumdrops, and costume jewelry on the floor, examining their labels and reading the offending bits aloud. "Thee?" he said. "The third ingredient ith melamine. That causes kidney failure." Or "Made in China. May contain radioactive waste." When he was done he packed it all into a plastic bag, tied a bit knot in the top, and said, "Thorry, kids. Thith thtuff could kill you. I'll make you Th'mores instead."

"Give it to me," Johnny said from the bunk where he was now popping three of Mr. Faber's red decongestant tablets. "I'll sell it to the old folks at the Home. They won't care."

As the bus filled up, the crowd spilled out the emergency door in the back into what Ti liked to call "the park." This was a weedy spot between the bus and the nursing home's loading dock where nobody ever went, except to dump old tires and broken couches. It was completely hidden from view. The Fabers had cleared out an area there, and built a lean-to and fire pit.

Eagle lit the torches while Dixon and Ti built a campfire and set up the tripod. His father then directed Dixon in the fine points of an old Faber tradition: the gumbo pot. They hung an enormous kettle from the tripod and tossed in onions, peppers, herbs, and water.

The scent began to travel o the basements, refrigerator boxes, and cars throughout this part of East Westford where people lived, and the word went around that there was a party, and it had food.

People brought the little bits of provisions they'd been hoarding and dropped them into the pot. Johnny Boots donated a rabbit he'd smoked himself. Heather Gaga dropped in a load of dried tomatoes. Hippy Dave added okra. Anna brought a catfish she'd caught that morning. All night long, as the party grew, Dixon dished up bowls of Faber gumbo, and all night long the pot never ran out.

Some time around nine, with a yellow moon rising and the Big Dipper visible in the north, Mr. Faber rooted around under the bus and found his old guitar. He sat down on a log by the fire and started plinking out an Irish folk tune as best he could on the three strings. Eagle joined in, beat-boxing with his mouth and banging pencils on an old paint can. Christine had a harmonica. Hobo Keith found his accordion. Doc snuck back into the nursing home —he and Johnny were now out after curfew—and got his trumpet.

Johnny Fitziguzzi was so hopped up on the red decongestant pills he'd found in the bus that he looked like he'd been set on fast-forward. After listening to the jigs, blues, funk, and old swamp tunes for a while, he ripped off his disco shirt and jumped into the firelight. "I got a song for you lowlifes," he howled, his eyes wide and twitchy. "It'll give this shindig some class."

He turned to the musicians and said, "Do you freaks know how to play *New York, New York*? 'Cause I'm way better than Frank Sinatra."

They did. Johnny swayed around in front of the fire, crooned tunelessly into an imaginary microphone for much too long, forgetting the lyrics and making them up as he went along. "If I can make Times square, I'll make it anywhere, It's up to me, New York, New York." He scratched at his pale belly. "I don't wanna wake up in a bathtub that's fulla creeps. Top of the king, hill of the list, A1 steak sauce. My orthopedic shoes, are longing to say, New York, New York, they make a nice hotdog there, the Bronx is up and the Battery's down, it's a helluva town . . ."

As he babbled, spun, and danced faster and faster, the crowd laughed and cheered. Then it looked like he might fall into the fire and hurt himself, so Mr. Faber started everybody clapping and cheering. Johnny bowed and waved. He looked delirious not only with drugs and alcohol, but with happiness. "Ain't I good?" Johnny yelled. "I told ya I was good."

To change the mood, Hobo Keith started up a fast-paced Acadian tune, and Eagle's beat-boxing gave it a hip-hop flare, with Doc's trumpet adding the New Orleans funk. Now Ti jumped into the light by the fire and did one of his goofy dances, which he called the Charley Birdbath. He waved his arms and kicked his feet around, and a crowd of kids joined in.

Johnny staggered back into the empty bus to look for more of the red pills. While pawing through the corners of the candle-lit space, he came upon the load of fireworks the Fabers intended to deliver the next day to Parker Worthington.

"This oughta get the party started," he said, and hauled outside packages labeled "Sputnik Skyrockets" and "Jumbo Bad Boy Suicide Shells."

When the explosions started, all the dogs and several of the war-veterans ran for cover. One of the security drones from Brimmingham Academy hovered over the lot for a minute, then retreated back to its side of the fence. Coyotes howled miserably in the distance. As the rockets exploded into bright, sparkling balls of blue, white, and green, however, people came back out of hiding, sat down around the warmth of the fire, and assumed it was all part of the celebration. They huddled with their friends, looked upward, and oohed, aaahed, and applauded after each explosion.

When they heard the sirens getting louder, however, the crowd scattered for good. By the time the police Humvees had crashed through the brush and weeds to the front of their bus, nobody remained but Mr. Faber and his three sons. Two officers in black riot gear pointed shotguns at them while a third slipped plastic zip-ties onto the boys' hands.

"What's this all about?" Mr. Faber demanded. "We didn't set off those fireworks. Someone else did."

"Fireworks are legal, sir," said the officer who seemed to be in charge. "We're arresting your sons for a hand-guns violation."

"Hand guns?"

"That's right, sir."

"We don't have any guns. And even if we did, isn't there something in the Bill of Rights? A well-armed militia, and all that?"

"Oh, you can have 'em, sir. In East Westford you can buy 'em, and own 'em, and sell all you want, no matter how young you are. But these kids gave a handgun to a—" he checked a notebook in his shirt pocket "—Demeter Gargleoff, or something like that."

"So?"

"So he's pressing charges."

"For what?"

"As you ought to know, Sir, Section 26 Subsection 12 makes it illegal in the City of East Westford to knowingly own, possess, sell, give away, or in any way facilitate the existence of a firearm that is not in operable condition."

"That heater don't work?" Eagle said.

"No it does not," the officer said. "We tested it this afternoon, and the firing pin is bent."

"And that's illegal?" Mr. Faber said, incredulous. "What if you have an antique or something?"

"Of course it's illegal," the officer said. "Imagine this Mister Barbasol's situation. Suppose he needed to shoot someone, and his gun doesn't work? How's he supposed to protect his freedom?"

"Well, isn't that what the police are for? To protect us?"

By then, however, his sons had been locked in the back of the Humvee and it was driving away.

Chapter 29

"Oh, how lucky we are!" Ti said the next morning.

"Real electrithity!" Dixon agreed.

"This television machine," Eagle agreed, "is da bomb."

They were lying on old army cots inside what was once the Sands Argent Elementary School, a three-story brick building built a long time ago. Dixon had actually attended this school for two years; it was on their side of town.

In order to cut costs during yet another round of budget cuts, however, the superintendant of East Westford Public Schools had been forced to close this school and put its 400-plus kids into Burr Oak Elementary, where some of the classrooms now contained twice as many kids as chairs. He'd then sold Sands Argent to the Halibutton Corporation, which made a considerable profit for their shareholders by running it as a private jail.

When they brothers had arrived here the night before, the guards had handed them a brochure explaining the rates. It said that they would each be charged $10 in expenses per day for incarceration in "General Population," due in full before release. This would get them each two meals a day, two trips to the bathroom, and ten squares of toilet paper. If they wanted extras, they'd have to pay up front.

The Faber brothers had heard horrible stories from nearly everyone they knew about "General Population" at the Sands Argent Improvement Facility. It packed hundreds of prisoners into the school's former gymnasium, where it was rumored that several people died every week from trampling, malnutrition, and bites from rats the size of house cats.

Ti still had their roll of money in his shoe when they'd been arrested, so he paid an extra $20 per day for what the brochure described as a "Premium Deluxe Educational Residence, complete with radiator, individual sleeping surfaces, and color TV." The guards had led them to and locked them inside the school's former art room. It still had the posters of famous paintings on the walls that Dixon remembered, a color wheel, and inspiring slogans, such as "Art is Long, Life is Short." Student-made paintings and collages remained taped to the windows as if the classes had just ended yesterday. Dixon had looked around at all this and said, "Yippee! Can we finger-paint?"

When they'd awakened in the morning they'd discovered three other people in the room. One was a chubby old man with an Australian accent. An enormous younger man in a suit sat beside him, holding a pistol—this was his bodyguard. There was also a sweet, white-haired lady they recognized from Burr Oak Elementary, a First-Grade teacher named Mrs. Murphy.

She was sitting by one of the windows, knitting with two long pencils and bits of yarn and string she'd discovered in the supply cabinet.

"I'm making a blanket," she told them cheerily. "It gets quite chilly in here during the winter time!"

"You've been here since winter?" Ti asked.

Eagle looked at her with newfound respect. "What are you in for? Cappin' some porker?"

"Excuse me?"

"He means, 'What did you do?'"

"Well, that's a funny story," she said, smiling and straightening her yarn. "One day I was weeding my vegetable garden when I heard a terrible racket in my neighbor's yard, so I got out the ladder and I looked over the fence. And you wouldn't believe what I saw. There were two dogs fighting each other, and a crowd of men standing around them waving their arms and yelling. I assumed they were all shouting at the dogs to make them stop. Well I knew how to get dogs to stop fighting. I turned on my garden hose and I sprayed those dogs, and sure enough they stopped."

"Yeah?" Eagle said. "So what? We wanna know what got you busted."

"Busted?" she said, smiling at Eagle. "You have always had such a *unique* vocabulary, Eagle, even when you were in first grade."

"He wants to know," Ti explained sweetly, "why you were arrested."

"Well, young man," Mrs. Murphy said, "That's the funny part. It turns out those dogs weren't fighting by accident. They were fighting on *purpose*. It was perfectly legal. And all those men weren't yelling at them to stop, they were yelling out bets. And I had no business stopping them."

"Why not?"

"Well, it turns out that this was a very special dog fight, to raise money for a very important state senator named Steve Rex. And I ruined it! I also got some of those nice men all wet with my hose. Some of them had to get their suits dry-cleaned. I offered to pay for it, of course, but this Mr. Rex really rather insisted that I should be charged with assault. So here I am, back in school, spending time with you nice boys!"

"When do you think you'll get out?"

"Oh, that'll be up to the judge, I guess."

"You haven't had a trial yet?"

"Not yet, no."

"How long have you been in here?"

She peered through her glasses at one of the pencils she used as a knitting needle, counted the notches to herself, and after a while said, "326 days."

"Have you had a hearing?"

"Oh, I'm sure it'll be any year now."

"Who's your lawyer?"

"I don't know yet. He hasn't been in to see me. He's very busy, you know. He's all alone!"

"So who pays for the premium room?"

"My daughter, God bless her, had a little money saved up before she was laid off from the hospital. And I get a nice senior-citizen discount, thanks to AARP."

"No lawyer?" Ti said, worried. "I can't be convicted of a crime. It would ruin my chances of becoming president."

"President maybe, Mate," said the jowly Australian in the far corner, "but you can still become a CEO. I been convicted a plenty a crimes, and I still manage to run one a the biggest media companies in the world."

"So why you here, Yo?" Eagle asked.

"Oh, I'm innocent as a newborn babe," the man said. "A bunch of socialists claim I was wire-tapping celebrities, but I don't believe a word of it. I'll be out as soon as my lawyahs buy the place."

Sure enough, a few hours later the Australian and his bodyguard were ushered out of the room by a horde of men in fancy suits. Ti saw them a few minutes later outside the window, being driven away in black SUVs. That afternoon a worker with a bucket truck arrived and put up a new sign in front of the jail that read, "The Sands Argent Improvement Facility, Another Jobs Creator Brought to You by The Moordavort Corporation."

Sometime after sunset the guard cuffed the brothers and Mrs. Murphy together and led them down the hallway to the cafeteria, where they each took a paper plate onto which a woman in a hairnet had dropped a spoon of brown slop. Ti recognized her as one of the nice lunch ladies at Burr Oak Elementary, who sometimes gave him left-over bits of bread. He smiled at her and asked appreciatively, "What's on the menu tonight, Doris?"

She smiled back and said, "Ah, stuff we can't feed to the donkeys."

"There are donkeys here?"

"You don't wanna know."

Nonetheless the boys were otherwise thrilled with their new prison life. They missed their father of course, but their room had electric lights, a luxury they couldn't afford in their bus, and they got two meals a day without having to hunt or scrounge for it. Plus, their room had a machine they'd only been able enjoy through the windows of the Nursing Home, or as a special treat when visiting Johnny Fitziguzzi: a television. Eagle and Ti were both transfixed. They watched it from the time they awoke in the morning until Mrs. Murphy told them at night that it was time for them to turn out the lights and "let the Sandman whisk you off to sleepy-land."

Dixon, meanwhile, was excited to discover that the supply closet still contained art supplies. In the back of one shelf he found a coffee can filled with worn and broken stubs of colored pencils. Whereas ordinarily he could only draw in black and white—the only pigments or viewpoints allowed at the Rush Transpacific Pencil factory, where his father worked—this gave him the opportunity to use reds, blues, yellows, and various shades of gray. Plus, unlike in art class at Burr Oak, here he found a pad that contained actual paper.

Dixon drew all kinds of things: Portraits of Mrs. Murphy, still lives of the spiders and dead bugs he found in the corners, and detailed drawings of meals he hoped one day to create. "These are magnificent!" Mrs. Murphy told him. "Your talent with line and shadow reminds me of Rembrandt, Durer, and Da Vinci all rolled into one."

"There's no money in fine art anymore, I'm afraid," Ti had countered. "According to the television machine, the big money is in lottery tickets. It'd better if you spent your time drawing some of them."

"Yeah, Mang," Eagle had agreed. "You wanna make us some serious coin, draw us up some video games, like *World of Deathcraft.* Or maybe somethin' about the superiority of dogs.*"

"Not this again," Ti said.

Ti and Eagle had been arguing for days about the shows they'd been watching. Ti's favorite was called *Little Brother.* Twelve kids were locked into an apartment with unlimited quantities of food, heat, and clothing, and all they had to do, while cameras followed their every movement and conversation, was vote off one of them every week. The kids ended up doing horrible things to each other in order to survive—they repeated made-up insults they claimed one kid had said about another, they stole items and planted them in their victim's beds, and they poisoned the food of their rivals.

Ti thought it was brilliant. He said it gave him "new ideas for criminal enterprises."

Eagle, however, told him, "It's staged, mang. It's made up."

"What are you talking about?" Ti said. "If it's on the television machine, it has to be true."

"No it don't, Brah," Eagle said. "That show about the guy what wins a million dollar?"

"*I Love My Lottery?*"

"Yeah."

"Ain't no way they give a guy a million dollar. Ain't that much coin in the whole world."

"Yes there is," Ti said. "Otherwise they couldn't show it to us."

Eagle preferred *The Puppy Palace,* an ongoing beauty pageant for dogs who squared off in talent, dress-up, and bathing-suit competitions. Ti called *Puppy Palace* "infantile," a word Eagle did not understand, but he assumed from Ti's tone that it was not a compliment.

That day during the latest episode of *Little Brother,* a boy with red hair had taunted a little girl for refusing to eat her pizza, because it was too "cheesy."

"You're a baby," the red-haired boy had said. "You probably wear diapers."

"I do not," the girl had said. "You do."

The two of them had gone on like this for five minutes.

"Look at this crunk," Eagle said. "If that little brizzie was a dog, she clean her plate. You don't have to beg no dog to eat its food."

"That's because dogs will ingest anything," Ti countered. "They'll eat grass. Excrement. Their own vomitus. They're positively puerile."

This had given Dixon a brilliant idea for a cartoon. When he was done, he showed it to Eagle:

You never have to beg your dog to clean its plate.

Eagle loved it. He said, "Tha's snorkey, Mang!"

Ti said nothing, but Mrs. Murphy agreed. "It reminds me of Hogarth, Beerbohm, and Kliban, all rolled into one," she said. "Pure genius."

Dixon blushed.

He was just about to show them another one when they heard the door unlock. Four guards burst in wearing riot gear and carrying sticks.

"Aw right, prisoners," one of them barked through his gas mask. "Are you gonna come quiet, or do we get to beat you?"

"We'll come quietly!" Mrs. Murphy exclaimed.

"Not you, lady," the guard said. "You're paid up through March."

He pointed at the brothers, who had retreated to the far corner by the Porta-Potty.

"It's you three I want," he said. "Your money's run out, and the party's over. We're movin' you to General Population."

"Oh no," Ti said. They'd heard the screaming from below them every night, and the smells. "Isn't there something we can do to stay in here? Maybe we could work or something?"

"Unless you got cash, credit card, gold coins, American Express travelers checks, or Groupons," the guard said, "you're comin' with us."

Chapter 30

"Hey Rusty!" the guard yelled as he pushed the Faber brothers in the door. "Looks like you got a couple new footstools!"

The brothers had expected General Population to be horrible, but they weren't prepared for this. Under bright florescent lights, about 400 males of all ages sat packed together tightly on the former gym floor. They didn't look up from what they were doing, which seemed to involve tying knots with gimp. It smelled like the inside of a really sweaty sneaker that had stepped in dog-doo. And the walls that had once hung with championship sports banners were now bare, covered with barbed wire and electrified metal fence. A group of men wearing red bandannas were picking up bugs off the ground, tossing them against the wire, and watching them sizzle and cook. Then they'd smile and pop them in their mouths.

Rusty approached. He was about five feet tall and four feet wide, with red hair and red eyebrows. He was wearing athletic shorts, a red University of Louisiana T-shirt, and a plaid pork-pie hat. He smiled at the brothers and said in a Cajun accent, "How y'all are?"

"Um...good," Dixon said.

"Ah doubt that'll last too long," Rusty said. "You in ma world now, boys. Ain't that right, Jalapeño?"

A tall, muscled prisoner with a red bandanna over his shaved head said, "Tha's right, Boss. You in Rusty Carlson's world now. And you betta do what he say."

"Yo Brah," Eagle asked cheerily. "What happens if we don't?"

"Show him," Rusty said.

Jalapeño grabbed Eagle around the waist, lifted him up like he was a log, and carried him over towards a Porta-Potty in a corner of the gym where two more prisoners in red bandannas stood guard. One of them lifted the back of the potty while Jalapeño began to shove Eagle in head-first.

"Fine fine fine!" Eagle said. "I was just curious!"

After a signal from Rusty, they set Eagle back on his feet. He adjusted his hoody and scampered back to his brothers.

"Tell these heah stools the rules," Rusty said, and turned away. As he walked to the far end of the gym, the prisoners seated on the floor with their gimp parted before him like the Red Sea had parted for Moses.

"That area," Jalapeño said, "Is off limits to the likes of you."

He pointed to Rusty's compound in the far corner, which was surrounded by a rope fence and had a sign in front that read, "Ragin Cajins." Inside this section was another, very clean Porta-Poddy, the gym's only cots, a microwave, and a refrigerator.

Rusty was now sitting on one of those cots. He clapped his hands and yelled, "Cerveza!" A gang-member opened the fridge, pulled out a Coors Lite, cracked it open, and handed it to him.

"Footstool!" Rusty yelled. A skinny boy with blonde hair ran over and kneeled in front of him. Rusty put his feet up on his back, downed the beer, tossed the empty can on the floor, sighed contentedly, leaned back, and began to snore.

In a remarkably high and polite voice, Jalapeño assigned each Faber to a gang-member for their own foot-stool duty. He explained to them that if they obeyed Rusty's gang, the Ragin' Cajuns, they'd get their two meals a day, two potty visits, and ten pieces of toilet paper. The first time they broke the rules, he said, they'd lose their food. The second time they'd lose their toilet paper, and the third time they'd lose use of the potty.

"Yo, what about the fourth time, Brah?" Eagle asked.

"The fourth time we feed you to the donkeys."

"Got it." Eagle said. "Donkeys."

"You!" Jalapeño said, pointing to Ti. "How old are you?"

"Eight," Ti said.

"Then your quota is eighty rings." Another gang-member used a black magic marker to write a big "80" on Ti's forehead. "You!" He pointed at Eagle. How old are you?"

"Ten?"

"I don't believe you. Your quota is one hundred twenty." The other guy knocked off Eagle's flat hat and drew a "120" on his forehead. On Dixon they wrote "140."

"Now get to work," Jalapeño said, and pointed them towards a pile of gimp in the middle of the gym.

"You got off easy," said a smiling old man with a faded "820" in the middle of his forehead. He was weaving and knotting the multicolored strands of plastic gimp so fast his fingers blurred. "I gotta make two of these key rings every three minutes."

"Do you?" Dixon asked.

"Sometimes," the old man said.

"What happens when you don't?"

"You heard the man," the old fellow said. "Haven't had food for three days."

"Are they going to throw you to the donkeys?"

"Not for a while, I don't think," said the old man, who told them his name was Roberto. "I may not do 82 an hour, but even on a bad day I'm pumping out 600 or so total, and that's earning Rusty and his Cajuns a lot of dough."

"How?" Ti asked.

"Didn't you know?" Roberto said, his fingers flying. "They've got a racket going with the guards. They sell these things on that website Etsy as handcrafted by genuine American artists. The guards keep the money, and the Cajuns get to eat good food. And every time we make another five hundred thousand, we get three hours vacation and day-old doughnuts. Doughnut Days are a lot of fun, lemme tell you."

He tossed a lovely pink and black key ring into a bin and looked up at the clock. "Okay, just 9 more in the next 14 minutes and I get food today."

At five o'clock they could hear the bolts opening on the other side of the doors, and noticed a general rustling of excitement throughout the gym. The gang-members gathered around the door. When it opened, the guards passed them a grey, plastic trash barrel.

The gang then required each prisoner to line up with his bin of key-rings, and if their bin contained the same number written on their forehead, they were sent to the food pail.

Because it was their first day, the Fabers were allowed to eat. When they got to the front of the line, a Cajun slopped a pile of brown goo into their cupped hands. It tasted like stale crackers mixed with grease and sand.

"Not exactly a big night out at Denny's," said their new friend Roberto, "but you get used to it."

"Oh, I've had way worth than thith," Dixon said.

"From where?" Roberto asked. "A dumpster?"

"Nope," Dixon said. "From a thchool."

Chapter 31

Things did not go well for Ti, however, over the next several weeks. Try as he might, he could not master the art of gimp. He'd cross the red over the green when he was supposed to twist it under, or tie a knot where he was supposed to make a loop. He gimped away all day long, and his brothers did extras for him, but for seven days straight so many of his key rings were rejected by the gang members that he was denied food.

"This could be you next!" Rusty yelled at him one morning, as they prepared to throw a prisoner to the donkeys. The poor man had worked in a meatpacking plant before he was arrested for stealing scraps to feed his family, and his fingers were so stiff and swollen with scars that he hadn't been able to produce the 450 daily key-rings required. The Cajuns stacked their cots until they were above the electric wires and able to reach the open windows near the top of the ceiling, then hauled him up. To Ti it didn't seem like the man was all that sorry to go. He waved to the crowd from the top of the cots and yelled "So long, Suckers!" as they tossed him through.

Ti was beginning to starve. His arms looked like sticks, and some days, even though his brothers tried to sneak him extra food, he felt too weak to tie any gimp at all. Dixon managed to catch some of the massive flies that buzzed around them and the scorpion-like bugs that scuttled across the floor, but so did everyone else, and it just wasn't enough nourishment.

One morning Ti left the Cajun Compound after foot-stool duty so weak he could barely walk over to the gimp. When he got there he collapsed onto Dixon and passed out.

"Wake up, Brah!" Eagle yelled in his ear, but Ti didn't move.

Dixon said, "Ti, Thweetie, are you okay?" When Ti didn't respond Dixon said to Eagle, "He needth food."

"Yo Cajuns!" Eagle yelled at the nearest gang-member. "My brah is dyin' here!"

Rusty sauntered over, wearing a black New Orleans Saints T-shirt. "How y'all are?"

Eagle pointed to Ti and said, "Bad. We gots to get him to the infirmary, stat!"

"You say he sick?"

"Yeah, Brah!"

"You got insurance?"

"No."

"Well medical don't come fa free here at da Sands Argent Improvement Facility." He pulled a brochure from the back pocket of his enormous jean-shorts. "Say right hyah, 'Transportation from General Population to Nurse's Office, Ten Dollars, Cash in Advance.' You boys got dat?"

"We ain't got diddly-squat," Eagle said.

"In that case then," Rusty said, "I won't waste my time readin' y'all the price list for treatment." He pointed to one of the pages. "Some a this ain't cheap. You want a band-aid, thas ten dollah. You want a Ibuprofin, fifteen dollar. An' an actual examination by a nurse's assistant? Hooo-ey. Two *hundred* dollar. Cash. Up front. And my end on top dat. Man, these Hallibutton, they know how to make some coin."

Rusty tossed the brochure at them. "Course, one a y'all can always sell yourself to that hospital they got ovah they to Brimmingham, for doin' experiments on. They pay three-hundred I hear. Thas good money. Think about it." He walked away.

Ti's eyes fluttered, then closed.

While Dixon held him and wept, carefully aiming his tears so they'd drop into Ti's mouth and possibly nourish him, Eagle worked the crowds of inmates for scraps of food.

"C'mon, Yo," he said to Louis, a gang-member. "Ain't I been a good foot-stool for you? Can't you spare my brah one a them Twinkies you got lyin' around your compound?"

Louis laughed.

When Eagle returned, Dixon said, "Hith pulth is dropping."

"Find me somethin' sharp," Eagle said. "I'm gonna open a vein and feed him my blood."

Just then a tone sounded that signaled an announcement from the guards outside the door.

"Attention, Improvement Guests!" said a charming female voice over the loudspeakers. "We have a visitor!"

A murmur of voices ran through the gym. "Someone's getting a visitor!"

"A visitor!"

Most of the prisoners had been here for years without a visit from a loved one. The jail charged visitors $150 per "guest" visited, money most of their relatives didn't have. The Faber brothers hadn't even had a letter from their father. He'd written them every day, but hadn't realized that he was supposed to pay the jail five dollars each to deliver them to his sons.

"The following three Improvement Guests will please report to the Welcome Center immediately."

"Three!" murmured the crowds. That was a lot of money. A rich person must be visiting, possibly somebody rich enough to pay for a lawyer, and a courtroom, and the jail bill, that could lead to an actual release. And, rumor had it, visitors were allowed to bring food.

The charming voice said, "Guest number 4163 Quebec Zero Niner! Please report to the Welcome Center to greet your visitor!"

Roberto, the nice old man next to them, looked at the ID tag that had been attached to the back of Eagle's ear. "Close, young man, but no cigar. You're Zero Eight."

Eagle looked at Dixon's ear tag. "He's Niner!"

"The kid's got Bingo!" Roberto said.

Dixon stood up. "Thath me!" he screamed. "But I'm not going without my brother. He'th thick!"

"Guest number 4163 Quebec Zero Eight!" said the charming woman. "Also report to the Welcome Center!"

Eagle pumped his fist in the air and yelled, "Snorky!" Then he looked down at Ti, who lay on the floor, pale and waxy. "But not without my little homey."

"And our final guest for today," said the perky announcer voice, "Is guest number 4163 Quebec Zero . . ."

"Thay theven!" Dixon whispered aloud, reading Ti's ear tag.

". . . Six!" said the woman.

A man in a kilt jumped up and yelled, "Aye! A visitor!"

"Shayam," Eagle said, as he watched the kilted man run towards the door. "Dixon! Rip this tag out my ear and stick it on Ti."

"No," Dixon said. "I'm gonna rip out mine." He was tugging on the ID tag when the tone sounded again and the charming voice said, "Correction!"

The kilted man stopped in his tracks. "What?"

"What?" Dixon said, and stopped trying to rip his earlobe apart.

"That last number was incorrect. My apologies! The correct number should be! Guest number 4163 Quebec Zero Seven. Have a nice day!"

The kilted man collapsed onto the floor, pounded it with his fists, and cried, "Boil yer bloody heads!"

The doors flew open, shots fired, and tear gas canisters exploded around the gym. Three guards entered in full riot gear, whacking anyone they could with sticks, while other guards using handheld tracking devices identified the Faber brothers by their ear tags.

The guards surrounded the brothers and whisked them to one side of the gym. One of the guards inserted a key in a switch, which shut off the power to a grid of the electric wall, then unlocked a door into a tiny room that had once been the gym teacher's closet. The Fabers were tossed on the floor. The door closed and locked behind them.

When Ti's eyes stopped tearing, he could see someone looking down at him.

It was Castelli.

"Here," she said, and handed them a paper bag. "It's food."

Dixon took it and found a bag of muffins inside. He ripped it open, crumbled a handful, and carefully inserted bits into Ti's mouth.

Eagle, meanwhile, had found a container of orange juice, which he unscrewed and held to Ti's lips. The smaller boy swallowed, then swallowed some more. Three more handfuls of muffin and he opened his eyes.

"Food." He smiled.

The three brothers devoured everything in the shopping bag Castelli had brought them so quickly that all they could remember later was that one second they saw lots of potato salad, sandwiches, and muffins, and the next second all they saw were empty containers and a very puzzled look on Castelli's face. As they licked the wrappers and then the paper bag she stared at them as if they were ferocious animals.

"Wow," she said. "That didn't take long."

"Thank you tho tho much, Madam Castelli," Dixon said, bowing before her. "You thaved my little brother's life."

"Yeah, thanks Lady."

"Why are you here?" Ti asked.

Castelli smiled mysteriously. "Because I overcharged you."

"In honor of thaving us," Dixon said, kneeling, "I would like to prethent you with thith thmall token of my eternal love." He pulled the drawing pad from the back of his pants, where he'd been hiding it, and handed it to her.

Castelli opened it, and flipped through the pages. "Hey," she said, laughing. "These are good. Dogs are definitely better than kids."

"Told you!" Eagle said.

She kept flipping the pages and laughing. "Wow," she said at last. "I love this."

"Lemme see!" said a voice the Faber brothers had come to hate. They turned.

Behind them, Rusty was standing in the doorway, holding a machete. "Ain't y'all gonna at least offer me a snack?"

"Sorry," Castelli said politely. "But I'm afraid the picnic is over."

"I wanna see them pictures," Rusty said. "I wanna see what so damn funny. You people makin' fun a Rusty?"

"No, thir," Dixon said.

Castelli looked at Rusty and held the book to her chest. "I'm so sorry to disappoint you," she said, "but these are mine, and I'm very bad at sharing."

In an instant Rusty had grabbed Ti from behind and wrapped his thick arm around the boy's neck. He held up the machete. "Show me the book, Missy," he growled, "or this little foot stool goes to the donkeys."

"Oh, all right," Castelli said. "I'll show it to you. I guess I should be glad that you're such an art lover."

"Madam Cathtelli thinks it's art!" Dixon whispered to Eagle.

Who responded, "Shut it."

Castelli walked towards Rusty, holding the sketch book out in front of her.

Just as Rusty reached for it, Castelli grabbed his wrist with her free hand, bent it down hard, and flipped it behind his back. The machete dropped to the tiled floor with a clatter.

Ti escaped safely to a corner of the room. Rusty was leaning forward, his arm twisted awkwardly, Castelli's knee pressed into his ribs. The book lay open on the floor.

"A little more pressure," Castelli said to him through gritted teeth, "and your arm will pop out of the socket. Sound good?"

"This *real* good," Rusty said, looking at a drawing in Dixon's book. He gave off a satanic cackle. "You right! A dog will definitely not text and drive. I text and drive once, I hit three nuns."

"Ith that what you're in jail for, Mithter Carlson?" Dixon asked.

"Na," he said. "I replace the stop sign in front of my house one time. Got tired a all them car crashes wakin' me up at night. Cops find out, take me in for unauthorized construction of a traffic device. Judge say I'm creatin' unnecessary government regulation, an' he wish he could give me the 'lectric chair. I been here ever since. It's startin' to feel like home."

Castelli let him use his other arm to turn the page of Dixon's book.

Rusty laughed. "You right again! You cain't walk your kid on a chain or people look at you funny. That happen to me!"

He turned a few more pages, admired a few more cartoons, and laughed some more.

"I tell you what," Rusty said. "This nice lady put my arm back in its socket, you not makin' gimp no more. You my artist. You in my gang."

"We can be criminals!" Ti said excitedly.

Dixon asked, "Can I bring my brotherth?"

"Sure, kid," Rusty said. "Sure."

Chapter 32

"Now I've just gotten feedback from the gang committee on your last comic," Jalapeño was saying to Dixon, "and they brought up some really excellent points. You say that a dog would never steal your credit cards and fly to Vegas. Alex and Tricky Tommy, however, pointed out that a dog can't steal your credit cards, because it doesn't have fingers. And without fingers, you'd never be able to remove the credit cards from a person's wallet. So they'd like you to change it to something a dog could steal, such as a ham bone."

Inside the gang's compound, Jalapeño had his feet up on the back of a prisoner named Jeff, while Dixon sat on the floor on the other side of the cot that served as Jalapeño's desk.

"A dog will never thteal your ham bone and fly to Vegas? That's what you think it should thay, Mister Jalapeño?" Dixon said.

"Yeah."

"Yo, Mang," Eagle said. He was sitting on the floor behind Dixon. "That ruin the whole point."

"It doesn't even make sense," Ti agreed. "As far as I know, airlines will not allow you to pay for plane tickets with a ham bone."

"The comic strip be called 'Doggy Better Yeah!', Yo,'" Eagle said. "So the point ain't that a dog could steal your credit card. The point be that a *kid* could steal it, but a dog can't, so dog better than kid. Get it?"

"No." Jalapeño pointed to Eagle and Ti. "You two footstools aren't even cartoon committee members. You weren't invited to this meeting, were you? Did I Entourage you? No. So scram. Get back to work."

Eagle and Ti reluctantly stood and went back to the gray plastic trashcan in the corner, where they did the gang's laundry. While Eagle rung rinse water out of socks and boxers, Ti hung them to dry on the gym's only radiator.

Dixon and Jalapeño, meanwhile, sat there for a while, looking at each other.

"So we want a hambone instead of a credit card," Jalapeño said after a while. "Do you understand?"

"No," Dixon said honestly.

"Why not?"

"I jutht don't."

Well, why not?"

"I don't know."

"I want you to change it to a hambone."

"Okay, I will."

"Do you understand why I want you to do that?"

"No."

Why not?" Jalapeño's voice grew louder, and his face red.

"What?"

"Why don't you understand?"

"I don't know," Dixon said. "I jutht don't."

"Why *not*!?"

"I don't *know*. I gueth I'm just a deeply flawed human being."

"That's *it*," Jalapeño said, enraged. "You have disobeyed me for the last time. I'm going to report you to gang management, and you're going to get a letter in your file."

Eagle, who had been listening to this from the wash corner, muttered to Ti in a fake slave voice, "Not that, massah. Whip me, sell me up the rivah, jus' don't put a lettah in ma file."

Ti giggled.

Gang life hadn't gone as planned. The brothers liked the food from McFatburgers three times a day (although Dixon complained about what all those trans-fats were going to do to their arteries), and not having to make gimp. But they still had to work as foot-stools and do all the gang's cleaning.

Plus, they missed their father.

And they could tell from the cold and the snow that sometimes blew in the windows at night that it was winter now, which meant they'd probably missed Smilus. The Faber brothers couldn't remember ever celebrating Christmas, Chanukah, Solstice, or Kwanzaa, but they had always loved the holiday their father had invented, called Smilus. It came on December 28th, the third day after Christmas. They got to pick out presents for each other, wrap them up, put them under the Smilus Stick, and open them on Smilus morning.

The presents were possible because in East Westford, the people who did receive presents on Christmas returned many of them to Wally World the following day. This meant that Wally World ended up with hundreds of tons of fairy tents, foot massagers, and other merchandise, which they couldn't resell, so they tossed them into the dumpsters behind the store. Early on the morning of the 27th, which the Fabers called Smilus Eve, they would climb into the dumpsters, select gifts for each other, and wrap them up in newspaper.

After they opened their presents on Smilus morning, the Fabers would celebrate the Feast of the Reduced, gorging on bags of red-and-green-wrapped Reese's Peanut-Butter Cups, Christmas cookies, and chocolate Chanukah coins that their parents had bought from Wally World's fifty-percent-off bin on December 26th. Then they'd burn the Pictures of Karma Cleansing and go outside for the Spreading of Smilus, the Ringing of the Bells, and the Carols of Cuss. For Smilus Vacation they'd visit a place they never been before. It was their favorite day of the year, and for the first time in their lives they'd missed it.

And Dixon wasn't enjoying his work at all. Rusty had once been a magazine editor, so he had created a complicated system for cartoon creation that everyone found confusing. First Dixon was supposed to submit an idea on a "pink sheet" to Jalapeño, who would come back to him with "suggestions." Once he'd made those changes he was to submit the revised idea on a blue sheet to a committee of gang-members, who made more suggestions he then had to include. When it finally got to Rusty on a yellow sheet, Rusty hated all the things Jalapeño had suggested, and the whole process began again. They had yet to finish a cartoon. For the first time in his life, Dixon felt stress.

Because Dixon was stressed, he couldn't sleep at night. Sometimes when he did fall asleep he'd have bad dreams and cry out, "I'm thorry thir, I didn't know the third rewrite went on a purple sheet, I'll never make that mistake again," or "I want a thalad!" This would awaken Shrimpy, a gang-member and light sleeper. He'd smack Dixon and yell, "Shad ap!" This generally woke Rusty, who was so annoyed he'd rouse the whole gang and demand that they come up with three new cartoon ideas that night.

After a while, Dixon found he could no longer draw at all. At the end of the day Jalapeño would demand to see what he'd completed, and most days it was nothing. "Do you want another letter in your file?" Jalapeño would say.

"No thir."

"Then you'd better give me twice as much tomorrow. Because I *know* you don't want another letter in your file."

Eventually, however, Dixon did get another letter in his file, and another, and then he had to have a private meeting with Jalapeño and Rusty. Rusty demanded to know why he wasn't producing more ideas and comics, and when Dixon said he didn't know, Rusty decided to cut his food allowance.

Still Dixon couldn't draw.

So Dixon got more letters in his file, and another meeting, and then Rusty cut his brothers' food allowance too.

Still nothing.

The brothers were starving again.

One night in the gang compound the Ragin' Cajuns celebrated Rusty's birthday and got extra drunk on Coors Lite. This gave Dixon an opportunity he'd been waiting for. When everyone was snoring loudly, he grabbed one of the cat-sized rats that regularly fed in the gang's trash barrels and expertly snapped its neck.

"Thorry, Rat," he whispered.

After skinning and gutting the rat with his fingers—he'd done this hundreds of times back at the bus—he placed it in the paper food bag Castelli had given them, along with salt he'd hoarded and some mushrooms and lichen he'd picked from the gym's walls and floor. He very quietly removed the vent valve from the side of the radiator, causing steam to shoot upwards. He covered this with the bag, and in fifteen minutes he'd produced a succulent meal.

He gently awakened Ti and then Eagle, and fed them bits of meat until they all felt full. "That was delicious, Dixon," Ti had whispered. "Thank you."

"Where that smell be at!?"

Rusty was standing over them, wearing nothing but a tight, orange pair of Texas Longhorns briefs.

"Uh," Dixon said, "Rattuth Maximuth Thteamed in Parchment? I'm afraid it's all gone, but I'd be happy to make you another, although I am running a bit low on lichen."

"You steal my rat?"

"I'm thorry, sir, I didn't know they were yours."

"Everythin' in here mine! This the last straw, boy. Tomorrow morning I call you up before the Human Resources Committee."

And he did. Rusty sat behind a cot on a human chair named Tim, surrounded by Jalapeño and the rest of the gang's leadership. After much arguing back and forth about the minutes from their last meeting, the correct interpretation of Robert's Rules of Order, and whether or not a motion to begin had to be seconded by one gang-member or two, the Human Resources Committee of the Ragin' Cajuns Prison Gang agreed to threaten Dixon with Death by Donkey if his comic production didn't increase immediately.

"If I may, your honors," Ti said, standing up before them as Dixon's lawyer.

"What it be, Stoolie?" Dusty demanded.

"Sir, I'd like to request on behalf of my brothers and me that you just go ahead and throw us to the donkeys immediately, sir. We've lost the will to live."

"No," Rusty growled. "Nobody git thrown to the donkeys for free. You wanna die, you gotta pay the rate."

"And how much would that be, sir?"

"Ten dollah per prisoner," Rusty said. "Cash. No checks, and no IOUs."

Ti bent down, removed one of his enormous shoes, lifted up the newspaper he used as an insole, and removed a little wad of green. He unfolded it, placed it on the cot, and said, "This is all we've got. How about a package deal? Twenty-two dollars for the three of us."

Rusty banged the beer can he used as a gavel on the head of Brent, the prisoner who served as his desk, which made a loud thumping sound. "You got a deal."

Chapter 33

"Furthermore," Ti was saying, "I'd like to point out that turkey vultures are truly an amazing creature. They're a misunderstood species that play a vital role in the web of life, and I think they would make great pets."

"Yeah yeah," Rusty said, looking at his watch. "Speed it up, will ya kid? In five minutes I got a meeting of the Energy and Commerce Committee, an' I ain't even read the minutes from last week."

"But Mister Carlson," Ti said, raising his little index finger. "These are my last words. I want to get them right."

Ti, Eagle, and Dixon were standing at the top of a stack of cots, facing the open windows of the gym. The air that blew in their faces smelled fresh, like spring and new leaves. Below them they could see a sea of prisoners staring up at them while hard at work on their gimp.

Ti had begun his speech thanking his parents, and his brothers, and several of his favorite teachers, whom he described in detail. He then veered off into a long lecture about the Stock-market Crash of 1929, FDR, Keynesian economics, government debt, and car headlights.

"I would also like to add," he continued, as Eagle and several of the gang members yawned, "that I have great regrets at all the things I wasn't able to do during my short life. I'm sorry that I never became the head of my own hedge fund, or the mastermind of a criminal enterprise. I wish that I could have bought my brothers an enormous house with a swimming pool and electricity, and that I could have taken my father to a board-certified allergist."

"Thirty more seconds," Rusty growled.

"And I regret that I have but one life to lose for my country."

"You ain't losin' it for ya country," Rusty said. "You losin' it for donkeys." He signaled to the gang-members who stood behind the Fabers at the windows. "Okay, boys. Give 'em a shove."

Jalapeño and two of his assistants—Shrimpy sat in a heap down below, sobbing at the loss of his favorite foot-stool—each grabbed a Faber by the back of their pants, hoisted them up, and lifted them into the windows.

"Ooh, how ironic," Ti said, pointing out over the rooftops of the jail. "I see a turkey vulture!"

The gang-members were just about to push when that tone sounded again throughout the gym, and the charming female voice came over the loudspeakers: "Attention please, Improvement Guests! We have a visitor!"

A visitor? Twice in one year? Prisoners below and the gang-members on the cots murmured amongst themselves. Who could it be, with so much money? A CEO? The Koch brothers? A king?

"Would the following guests please report to the Welcome Center to greet your visitor! Guest number 4163 Quebec Zero Niner! Please report to the Welcome Center to greet your visitor! Guest number 4163 Quebec Zero Eight! Please report to the Welcome Center to greet your visitor! Guest number 4163 Quebec Zero Seven! Please report to the Welcome Center to greet your visitor!"

It was the three Faber brothers. Again!

"Oo ye yi!" Rusty wailed. "I'm never make this meetin'.'"

Again the doors of the gym unbolted from the outside, and the prisoners covered their faces when the doors burst open and the tear-gas bombs exploded over their heads. The guards rushed in wearing riot gear, smacking anyone they could with black sticks until they'd found the Fabers via the tracking devices and dumped them inside the little room.

Again, when the brothers' eyes cleared, they were looking up at Castelli.

"You look ravithing today, Madam Cathtelli," Dixon said dreamily.

She seemed mystified by this; she was wearing her usual red high-top sneakers with paint-covered jeans and cap with a big green lizard on it.

"If you don't mind," Ti said to her politely, "can we make this quick? We're kind of in the middle of something right now. I'm saying my last words."

"Well that sounds good and jolly," Castelli said, smiling for only the second time in their experience, "But first I have some news for you that you might like."

She pulled an envelope from her pocket, removed a folded set of papers, and laid them out before them. "This is a contract. If you sign it, we can pay off your jail bill, get the charges dropped, and free you today. And you'll still have about ninety grand in your pockets."

"Okay," Eagle said.

"Hold on," Ti said. "What's going on here?"

Castelli explained that she had brought Dixon's book of drawings home to her house and enjoyed them very much, especially the cartoons about kids and dogs. While she was chuckling over the cartoons, a friend of her step-father had happened to visit, a Mister Harold Crump, who she said was a publisher in New York. Mr. Crump had also loved the cartoons, and wanted to sell them as a book called *Doggy Better Yeah!* "Dogs are very big right now," he had said. All they had to do was sign this contract, which would pay them 99 thousand dollars for the rights, and he'd pay for them to be freed immediately.

"All right," Ti said, looking over the contract. "This looks acceptable to me. But before we leave, I'll need to finish my speech."

Chapter 34

"This is gonna be the best Smilus *ever*," Ti said a week later.

"Yeah," said Dixon. "What time doeth the fine dining ethtablishment open?"

"Eleven o'clock," their father told him yet again.

"Okay, good," Eagle said, "Cause we still got lots of kareemy stuff to do."

The Faber brothers had already done a lot since they left jail. They had paid their jail bill with the book money. Then they had done as the judge had ordered and gone down to Liberty Shoot N Stuff, where they bought a brand new Smith and Wesson M&P semi-automatic .40-caliber pistol. They insisted that the owner prove to them that it worked, so he took them down to the range in his basement and fired off 17 shots in about three seconds.

Then they took this gun to the apartment of Dimitri Gerbatov. After twenty minutes of pleading through his heavily armored door, they managed to convince him that they were giving him this gun in order to get him to drop the charges against them, not because they intended to shoot him. The lawyer Castelli had found them insisted that Gerbatov sign a release form, guaranteeing that he was satisfied with the condition of the gun and would drop all charges against them. First, however, Gerbatov demanded that they pay him an extra $1500 so he could buy a freezer and 52 whole turkeys. When they handed over 30 crisp fifty-dollar bills, he signed.

Their first day of freedom, Ti also authorized what he called "capital improvements." They bought their father a year's supply of allergy medicine, a hypoallergenic pillow, new strings for his guitar, a gas mask to wear at work, and a wood stove that didn't leak smoke into the bus. They also bought each of them an electric blanket, and hired their friend Dave to install a solar system on the roof of the bus. Now they were warm and toasty, and their father was finally sleeping at night.

Ti had also allowed each of them to buy a special treat. After Eagle said he wanted a submarine so he could smuggle in drugs from Columbia, Ti gave them each a budget of a thousand dollars. Eagle blew most of his making a rap video with M.C. Larry. "Rap Supa Cool Dope," with its cheap lighting, muddy sound, and unintelligible lyrics, had already attracted 33 viewers and six comments on Youtube, all of them insulting. "So terrible I now hate all music," one of the kinder reviewers said. Said another, "I've got an ostrich that can barf out better beats than this." Eagle, however, was loving it. He told anyone who would listen to him, "I be famous, Yo. I got 33 fans."

Dixon had bought a mini-fridge, a top-of-the-line Weber kettle charcoal grill "which will allow uth to cook ribth and preserve foods by indirect thmoking," and a set of Sabatier chef's knives. He had gone right to work planning out a menu for the month. "On Tuesday the twenty-fifth," he'd said at one point, "would we rather have thalmon or lamb?" He'd thought for a second and then said, "Or we could have both!"

Ti had bought himself a set of business cards identifying himself as "Ticonderoga Faber, CEO." He also bought the newest Macbook, which he was able to power off the solar-electric system. The first time he turned it on to start his online Latin course he'd called to his brothers to come see the advertisement that had popped up on his screen. It was for a new book called *Doggy Better Yeah!*

"That'th our book!" Dixon said.

"Check it, Yo," Eagle said. "But how come this say it by Harold Crump, and not by me?"

"Who cares?" Ti said. "We got paid, didn't we? And with my investment strategy, soon we'll be millionaires."

They had also decided to have a really big Smilus. Today wasn't the third day after Christmas, when they usually celebrated it. December had long since passed, and the weeds and trees in their lot now sprouted shiny green leaves. But the beauty of inventing your own holiday, their father pointed out, was that you could celebrate it whenever you wanted. So they had decided to enjoy Smilus immediately. And now they had enough money to *buy* presents, rather than depend on the Wally World dumpster.

When they awoke Smilus morning, the brothers all smiled at the sight of the presents under the Smilus Stick. This stick had been Dixon's favorite pet when he was little, and was now worn smooth by over a decade of Smilus celebrations. As was the tradition, the night before they had not only placed their gifts to each other at its base, but decorated it with their Pictures of Karmic Cleansing.

When they'd opened all their gifts and the floor of the bus was covered with torn newspaper, Ti went to work organizing the contents of the new, leather briefcase his brothers had given him. Dixon set up his new drawing easel in one corner and started a pastel portrait of their father, who was reading the book they'd given him, called *Executive Job Search*. Eagle put on the shiny golden jacket he'd gotten, the matching golden basketball sneakers, and a flat-hat made of mink. He swished the air with his new black cane and said, "Check it, Homeys! There's a diamond in the top."

"And unlike your belt buckle," Ti said, "that diamond is real."

Next came the Feast of The Reduced. Traditionally this meant gorging on post-holiday items with marked-down prices, but there was no half-price candy at Wally World in April, so Dixon had purchased reduced-fat milk, reduced-salt Triscuits, and reduced-sugar Sugar Booms.

Then, one at a time, they took down their Pictures of Karmic Cleansing from the Smilus stick. The idea was to draw the person or thing that had bothered you the most in the previous year and get them out of your system by burning them up. In turn they each spat on their picture, tossed it into the fire, and watched it burn away into nothingness. It felt good.

Eagle had drawn his of Jonas, the second-grade bully who terrorized him on the bus. Dixon had drawn the music teacher at Hovering Parents Charter School, for forcing "innothent children to thing that terrible 'Each of Us is a Flower' tune." Their father, as usual, had drawn a picture of "Mister Rush-job," as he called the owner of the pencil factory who had failed to repair the machine that had killed their mother.

And Ti had simply written out the words "Trickle Down Economics." When it was his turn to burn he said, "Tax cuts for the rich didn't work the first time, so they tried it again, and that didn't work, so they tried it again, and it still didn't work, so they tried it again. Crazy."

Then they got all dressed up in the new outfits they'd bought at Salvation Army. Ti put on a new-to-him, white button-down shirt, and a vest and tie that hung to his knees. Dixon, now that he was a published author and artist, had bypassed his usual super-hero t-shirts for a tweed jacket and beret. Their father was wearing a black suit, and Eagle an extra-baggy pair of jeans covered with zippers and pockets and an actual chrome belt for his flashing "Im Ool" buckle.

Now it was time for the Spreading of Smilus. Before they'd had money, they would travel around their neighborhood, knocking on the boards under the bridges and the sides of old boxes where people lived, and given out compliments. They did this today as well, but with an added bonus. "Thanks for teaching us how to set snares this summer," they said to Ray Turtle. "You helped us survive."

"Your goiter is so much smaller," they said to Mr. Smith. "You look great."

"Thanks for being so happy all the time," they said to Mrs. Hazzard. She responded in her deep voice with what she always said to everyone: "I love you, da'lins."

Today, however, they also handed their neighbors the thing they knew they needed most: envelopes full of cash.

At the Nursing Home they told Doc he looked just like Chris Rock, who was his hero, and gave him an Eva Longoria poster. They thanked Johnny Fitziguzzi for being like a grandfather to them, and handed him an iPod loaded with Frank Sinatra music.

"What the heck is this?" Johnny said when he'd unwrapped it. "Why'd you give me a little metal box? You're rich now. Why couldn't ya give me something good, like a case of chocolate-whipped-cream flavored vodka?"

When Eagle turned it on for him, however, and put the headphone to his ear, Johnny smiled and said, "Not bad. Not bad. But he don't sing as good as me."

Next came the Ringing of the Bells. For this they all piled into their new "carriage." They'd built it by adding cushions and an old umbrella to Dixon's shopping cart, the one that was made to look like a little car. They tied the two used bicycles they'd gotten cheap at the pawn shop to its front. Ti squeezed in behind the little wheel, their father sat on the cushions in the cart, and Eagle and Dixon towed them with their bikes to Mill Street, the part of town where people in East Westford said the "rich folks" lived.

These were actually very small two-family houses occupied by people who had worked at the toothbrush factory before it closed, but they still got social-security checks so they seemed wealthy compared to a lot of people in town. Each house had a little patch of green grass in front, which sometimes inspired their proud residents to yell at children passing by on the sidewalk, "Git off a my lawn!"

While Mr. Faber hid behind the "carriage" at one end of the street and pretended not to know what was going on, the boys each snuck up to a doorbell, rang it, and ran away. Once they were safely out of sight, they laughed uproariously.

Next they performed the Carols of Cuss. They drove the carriage to their usual spot, an abandoned parking lot by the highway where the roar of cars was deafening. While their father plugged his ears, the boys were allowed to yell out all the bad words they could think of for five minutes.

"There," Ti said as he climbed back behind the little plastic wheel of the carriage-cart. "That ought to hold me for another year."

Chapter 35

Now it was time for Smilus Vacation.

One year they had ridden the bus for the first time in their lives and gone to West Eastford, a neighboring town. They spent an entire, glorious day inside a library, and it had books everywhere. Another year their father had somehow snuck them into North Southington, where they had visited a store called a "bakery," inhaled the delicious aroma of fresh bread, and each picked out their own pastry. The year before that they had spent their vacation at the "theater," which was actually the county courthouse, watching the trial of a high-school girl accused of not saying "under God" while reciting the Pledge of Allegiance. She got a year in Juvie.

This year, since they had money, they'd decided to do two fabulous things the boys had never tried before: eat at a sit-down restaurant, and stay somewhere overnight.

When they got to the finest restaurant in West Eastford, it had just opened.

Eagle sniffed the air, which smelled like frying, and said, "Yum!"

"Tables!" Ti said, looking around. "With napkins! And water glasses that they fill for you. This is so awesome!"

"Wow," Dixon said. He was looking with wonder at the water fountain in the lobby, where water trickled over polished black stones and bamboo. It didn't look like it had been cleaned in years—the bamboo was covered with green slime, and the water that had once contained gold fish now contained a few floating cigarette butts. "A water fall!" he exclaimed. "Indoorth!"

An Asian man in his sixties greeted them. He had a big square head and buzzed hair, dressed in a gray tunic and gold-framed Elvis glasses. Unbeknownst to everyone in West Eastford, he was an escaped North Korean dictator on the verge of bankruptcy. "Welcome to the Gung Ho Golden Buffet," he said. "Welcome! You skinny. That good."

Before Ti had finished paying for the four of them, Eagle had already grabbed a plate at the buffet and was stacking it with food.

"Check it, Homeys!" he said. "You gots your fried chicken, your fried waffles, your fried egg rolls, and it's all orange!"

"Please read signs," the man who had greeted them said. "You must eat bowl of rice with every item."

"Kareemy!" Eagle said.

The Fabers overloaded their plates with fried beef chunks in a sugary red sauce, fried dough lumps with specks of chicken inside, and fried wontons in a gooey yellowish soup. The place was already filling up, but they found a table in the back. The host, who introduced himself as General Kim, took their drink orders and came back with huge pitchers of watered-down soda. "Drink up!" he said. "All you want! Fill your belly!"

Their father picked at a greasy plate of lo mein, but the three brothers inhaled their food and kept going back for more.

"Check out the fried marshmallows!" Eagle said, stuffing a few in his mouth. "They snorky."

"I like the fried chocolate cake," Ti said.

Dixon was not happy about the high level of saturated fats, but he nonetheless ate everything he could. "What the heck," he said to himself. "It'th Thmilus Day!"

After each of the brothers had finished five plates and were piling up their sixth, General Kim came to their table and said, "You eating rice? You must eat rice!"

"Oh yes," Ti said. "The rice is delicious. I've already had seven bowls!"

"Aye yi yi!" General Kim said. "You pay $9.99, you eat $49.99. You make me broke!" He rushed off, his hands over his cheeks.

After two pitchers of orange soda, Eagle needed to use the bathroom. He found that it was locked. He asked General Kim for the key.

"So sorry!" the owner said. "Toilet broken."

"No problem, Yo," Eagle said. "I'm used to that crunk from jail. I can hold it for hours."

"Eat more rice!" Kim commanded as he handed the bathroom key to another customer with a much smaller appetite.

When the Faber brothers had finished their seventh plates, as well as three bowls of soft-serve ice cream, General Kim arrived at their table all smiles.

"Now that you full and ready to leave," he said, "I bring you special North Korean—I mean *Chinese* treat." It was a fried orange pudding that contained raw oatmeal, bloatner, and saw dust, something he'd specially formulated to expand in the stomachs of particularly expensive eaters and make them feel sick.

He watched the three brothers spoon it into their mouths and lick the bowls.

"Divine!" Dixon said a few minutes later. "Ith there more?"

"Shibal!" General Kim swore and strode quickly into the kitchen, where they could hear metal pans banging on the floor.

He got really upset around two o'clock, however, when Ti took out the Monopoly board.

"What you doing?" General Kim demanded.

"Playing Monopoly," Ti said. "It's quite lifelike."

"And it gives uth time to digetht," Dixon said.

"You cannot play game in restaurant! Is against law!"

"No it's not," Ti said.

His father added, "There's no sign."

"Yot Mogo," General Kim swore, and stormed off. Five minutes later he came back and tacked a paper placemat to the greasy wallpaper above their table. It read, "No Play Games."

"There!" he said. "You breaking rules! You want me call police?"

"Do the Jakes actually come when you call in West Eastford?" Eagle asked. "They don't in our town."

"Oh well," Dixon said. "If we can't play Monopoly, I gueth we'll have to eat more."

After they'd cleaned three more plates of orange-fried meat sticks, General Kim ran to their table with a worried look on his face. He pointed to the parking lot and said, "Oh no! Your car on fire!"

"We have a car?" Eagle said. "This I gotta see!"

"Oh no!" Dixon yelled. "My carriage!" They both ran out the door. There was no car fire, however, and their bicycle carriage was just as they'd left it.

When the two brothers tried to come back in, General Kim was there at the door. Another man in a grey apron stood behind him, holding a cleaver. The General said, "Sorry. Once you leave buffet, you cannot come back in."

"But you tricked us, Mang!"

"No trick! You must pay!"

"Okay," Dixon said, and handed him another twenty dollars.

After General Kim had watched them eat four more plates of fried rice, fried meat, and fried noodles, three more bowls of Jello covered with Kool Whip, six chocolate puddings, sweet potatoes with marshmallows, and a pile of fried bread, the owner came to their table, his face red.

"That it!" he yelled at the Fabers. "You fat Americans eat more in one day than my people eat in year! Get out!"

"But you told uth we were thkinny."

"And you're still open for six more hours."

"Get out or I send you to camp!"

Ti looked excited by this. "Latin camp?"

"You can't just kick us out," Mr. Faber said. "We're not doing anything wrong. It's all you can eat, and these boys can eat."

"Okay, fine, big shot," General Kim snarled. "I close restaurant. For good!"

He climbed on top of a chair. "Attention, subjects! Restaurant now closed by official decree! Everybody out!"

It took a while, during which time Eagle managed to shove nine more fried cheese balls in his mouth, but by four o'clock General Kim had cleared everyone from the restaurant, locked the door behind them, and flipped the 'Open' sign over so it now said 'Closed.'

"Perfect," Ti said, looking at the plastic watch he'd bought at Salvation Army. "It's time to check in to our motel."

The Fabers had heard the stories about the murders at the Bates Motel, but they didn't really care. None of them had ever stayed in a motel before, and it was tough to beat the price of $19.95. The room, when they entered it, smelled like mildew, and the floor was covered with a stained brown carpet full of cigarette holes. They thought it was fabulous.

"Beds!" Dixon said.

"TV!" Eagle said.

"Glasses covered with plastic! Free soap!" Ti said from the bathroom. "And all the toilet paper you want!"

"Hot running water," Eagle said. "I call first shower."

Dixon yelled, "I call second and fifth shower!"

"I call the Business Channel," Ti said.

"Aw," Dixon wined. "I wath hoping to catch *Primal Grill* on PBS."

"I wants my MTV!" Eagle yelled from the bathroom.

"I've got to watch the Business News," Ti said. "I need to complete my research on how to invest the rest of our funds. You do want to be millionaires, don't you?"

"I gueth," Dixon said.

While their father took a nap in the next bed, Ti clicked the remote and changed channels on the wall-mounted TV until he found the Business Channel. He lay back and watched while Dixon made a fort with the tattered bedspread and an old metal folding chair.

"C'mon, Brah," Eagle said when he'd finished his 45-minute shower and Dixon had replaced him. "Just a little MTV? The hip-hop awards are on."

"Funny you should mention hip-hop," Ti said, smacking his hand against an alternative newspaper he'd found on the side table, "because I just read that there's a night club in West Eastford."

"Get out," Eagle said. "Really?"

"Really. With music, and food, and ladies, and everything."

"Yeah," Eagle said, "But what kinda music? Some kinda folkie crunk? Some longhair with a guitar?"

"Not tonight," Ti said. "Tonight at Club Burner they've got DJ McSwagster."

"DJ McSwagster?" Eagle said. "Git out."

"And I think he's seen your video."

"You think?"

"What's thith?" Dixon emerged from the bathroom wrapped in a towel.

"We steppin' out to see some hip hop, Brah," Eagle said. "The peoples needs to see me."

"And I hear they serve an excellent fish taco at Club Burner," Ti said.

"Oooh!" Dixon said. "I'm thtarving!"

"Ah, Mang," Eagle said. "We ain't 21, and we ain't got no fake IDs."

"Not a problem," Ti said, pulling a few crisp 50-dollar bills from the briefcase. "Just give each of the doormen one of these."

When they were finally gone and their father was snoring in the other bed, Ti was able to concentrate on the Business Channel. He wanted to decide how best to invest the rest of their money. Around 8 pm a show came on that featured a bald man with frizzy orange side-hair and bug-eyes who screamed about stock tips. The show was called "Jim Wyndmoor is Crazy Rich!"

"That's what I want to be," Ti said to himself, and smiled. "Crazy rich."

Jim Wyndmoor stomped around, waved his arms, and yelled for a while at two guests in chairs who worked at major Wall Street banks. He then demanded they name good stocks to buy.

One of them mentioned Sefinex, which made Ti sit up in bed and pay close attention. He'd been watching this stock closely as a possible investment, ever since his accounting teacher at the church had mentioned it.

"Sefinex is garbage!" Tim Wyndmoor yelled at him. "Are you kidding me? They just came out with that new laser oven, and yeah it cooks a turkey in twenty seconds, but it also burns the meat!"

"I admit that they do have some problems to work out," the Wall Street woman said, "but at two dollars a share I think it's a very good deal. I could see it going to fifty in the next six months."

"Wrong!" Wyndmoor shouted at her. "You're an idiot! You'd be better off buying lottery tickets!"

The show went to a commercial, so Ti clicked the channel down one and happened upon the opening sequence of a show called "Lifestyles of the Lottery Winners." It was hosted by a little

English man who wandered through a fancy house talking to the owners, a couple who had allegedly won a lot of money in the lottery. He admired their indoor pool, indoor riding ring, and indoor miniature rhinos.

Then that show went to a commercial, which was a message from a wealthy man sitting in a Mercedes Benz who said he was the Merry Millionaire, and he owed it all to the Lottery Commission.

"Lottery tickets one second, and lottery winners the next? Three in a row?" Ti said to himself. "This is a sign."

Chapter 36

"What is this, some kind of a joke? Or are you gonna try to tell me you're making another movie?"

Sheila, the clerk at Bob's Kwikky Stop, was pointing her loaded shotgun right at Ti's face.

"No, no," Ti shouted over the loud Polka music. "I'm serious. We'd like 76 thousand lottery tickets."

"Yeah, right," Sheila said, and scanned the parking lot outside for video cameras. "This is one of them reality shows, isn't it? I'm about to get punked."

"No way, Sista," Eagle said. He was wearing his brand new, shimmery gold jacket and his hat made of mink. "We gots the Benjamins right hee." He placed a briefcase on the counter next to the Slim Jims, inserted a key, and popped the locks.

"Wow," she said.

"Seventy-six thousand," Ti said. "In actual cash. We want seventy-six thousand Instant Happiness Mega Billions tickets, please."

"Okay," Sheila said. "But this is gonna take a while."

"According to the Merry Millionaire," Ti had told his brothers that morning, "we'll be happy for life. I've worked out the odds, and we are guaranteed to turn our 76 thousand into 43 million in one day. It's fool-proof."

"Are you thure about that?" Dixon asked.

"It said so on the TV machine," Ti explained, "and the TV machine is not able to lie, because it's a machine."

"Snorky!" Eagle said. "Let's jet!"

So they had, down to Bob's Kwikky Stop, where they noticed that while they were in jail, Sheila had gotten a new tattoo on her forearm, this time of a weeping angel.

It took Sheila several hours to count out the tickets, while the Faber brothers munched on microwave chili dogs and big bottles of Moxie. When she was done she called the Brinks Truck, so that as soon as she took possession of the cash it could be safely whisked away to the bank. "This neighborhood ain't what it used to be," Sheila said.

The brothers filled their briefcase with the tickets and ran home. While Dixon grilled Cornell Chicken, Ti and Eagle sat at their table and scraped the grey wax off tickets. "Five dollars!" Ti yelled at one point.

"I got me a century!" Eagle yelled an hour later.

Worthless tickets piled up on the floor of the bus.

When they'd finished scraping late the following day, they had winnings that added up to $1,033, plus 3 coupons for half-off at a local nail salon.

Ti announced their next move. "I've calculated the odds," he said, "and our 43-million-dollar jackpot is right around the corner."

"Where?" Dixon asked, looking around the bus.

"Back at Bob's Kwikky Stop," Ti said.

The following day they skipped school and ran down to the Kwikky Stop. They cashed in the winning tickets, bought three more Moxies, a case of pork rinds, an order of deep-fried cheese-cake bites, an air freshener that smelled like ripe bananas, and 984 more Instant Happiness Mega Billions tickets. Sheila said she'd take the nail-salon coupons off their hands in trade for a large blue Slurpie. "I've been thinking about getting these painted up with some pink lady-bugs," she said, showing them the gnawed stubs of her nails.

Back in the bus, Ti sat over the pile of tickets. "This time," he said, "I'm using my lucky penny."

"Here we go," Eagle said. "Watch the dollah train come to town!"

By the time they were done scratching, the bus floor was ankle deep in discarded tickets, and they had 86 dollars worth of winners.

"I don't understand it," Ti said, punching buttons on his calculator. "The laws of statistics say we should have won over 30 million by now. The big tickets must still be at the store."

They raced back to Bob's, cashed in the winners, bought a box of chocolate covered marshmallows dipped in ice cream and rolled in sugar, and spent the rest on more Instant Happiness Mega Billions tickets.

Because this was a much smaller stack of tickets, they decided to scrape them on the toilet-paper vending machine outside the store. Even though Ti used his lucky penny again, and Eagle recited all of 50-Cent's "I Get Money," their 81 tickets yielded only six dollars in winnings.

"Shayam!" Eagle said. "I wants me some Instant Happiness, Brah!"

"It's all in those six tickets," Ti said. "It's got to be."

This time in the store, Eagle wanted to buy a bag of gummy dogs, but Ti said no. They bought six more Instant Happiness Mega Billions tickets, and this time scratched them right on the counter while Sheila hummed along to a polka tune.

Five of the tickets were duds. One of them, however, was a winner. It was worth a dollar.

When they'd bought that last Instant Happiness Mega Billions ticket, Ti wrapped it up in a tissue and locked it carefully inside the briefcase.

"This is it," Ti said. "This one's gonna be the golden ticket, just like Charlie Bucket. We are going to be rich now."

Back at the bus, Ti checked his Twitter account on his Macbook and discovered that Sefinex, the stock he didn't buy, had gone from two dollars a share to 53 in one day on news that their laser oven was ideal for removing tattoos. "Oh well," he said. "We're about to have Mega Billions."

Eagle took down a special candle from his shelf with the picture on the outside of Saint Mathew, patron saint of money. "Saint Matt, Brah," he said as he lit the candle. "I been savin' you for a special occasion. Now show us some love."

Ti, meanwhile, went through every good-luck charm listed on Wikipedia. He snapped a match for a "lucky break." He threw salt over his shoulder. He said a silent prayer to every god he could think of. He had Dixon, who was busy filleting a monkfish, kiss the ticket, then he kissed it himself.

When they finally felt ready, Dixon, Eagle, and Ti held the penny together.

"Are you ready?" Ti asked.

"Ready."

They scratched away the grey wax, and a long series of symbols revealed themselves on the ticket.

"Wow," Eagle said.

"Amazing," Ti said.

"What?" Dixon asked, struggling to read it. "What ith it?"

"A free tire rotation at Wally World," Eagle said.

"Cool!" Dixon said. "Doeth our buth thtill have tires?"

"It still has one tire," Ti said, "But we'd have to drive it there, and remember we sold the engine for scrap?"

"Oh yeah."

"Never mind," Eagle said, reading the lottery ticket closely. "It says here, this offer is expired."

"Dang," Ti said, and opened another bag of pork rinds. "It wasn't supposed to turn out this way."

"Oh well," Dixon said. "Let'th look on the bright thide." He gathered up handfuls of the thousands of lottery tickets on the floor of the bus, opened the door of the stove, and tossed them in. "Now we've got fuel for the next theveral dayth!"

The end.

(To be continued, in Books 2, 3, and 4!)

Please! Tell us what you think and how to make the Pencil Bandits better. Take the survey at http://www.surveymonkey.com/s/VZ7DCPW